STONE HEART

STONE HEART

A Novel of Sacajawea

DIANE GLANCY

THE OVERLOOK PRESS
Woodstock & New York

First published in the United States in 2003 by
The Overlook Press, Peter Mayer Publishers, Inc.
Woodstock & New York

WOODSTOCK:
One Overlook Drive
Woodstock, NY 12498
www.overlookpress.com
[for individual orders, bulk and special sales, contact our Woodstock office]

NEW YORK:
141 Wooster Street
New York, NY 10012

∞ The paper used in this book meets requirements for paper
permanence as described in the ANSI Z39.48-1992 standard.

Library of Congress Cataloging-in-Publication Data

Glancy, Diane.
Stone heart : a novel of Sacajawea / Diane Glancy.
p. cm
1. Sacagawea—Fiction. 2. Lewis and Clark Expedition (1804-1806)—Fiction.
3. Charbonneau, Jean-Baptiste, 1805-1866—Fiction. 4. West (U.S.)—History—
To 1848—Fiction. 5. Lewis, Meriwether, 1774-1809—Fiction. 6. Clark, William,
1770-1838—Fiction. 7. Shoshoni women—Fiction. 8. Explorers—Fiction. I. Title.
PS3557.L294 S7 2002   813'.54—dc21   2002030820

Book design and type formatting by Bernard Schleifer
Printed in the United States of America
ISBN 1-58567-365-X
1 3 5 7 9 8 6 4 2

For my daughter, Jennifer,
and her sons, Joseph
and Charles Brouillette

Foreword

Sacajawea was around sixteen, and pregnant, when Lewis and Clark met her in 1804 in the Mandan Village in North Dakota where they wintered. Her French-Canadian husband, Toussaint Charbonneau, had either bought, won, or somehow acquired her from the Hidatsa, who had adbucted her from the Shoshoni as a child. Both Charbonneau, an interpreter, and Sacajawea were chosen for the expedition that left Fort Mandan on April 7, 1805. None of Charbonneau's several other wives were included.

Sacajawea had given birth two months before the expedition left, and was intermittently ill on the journey and often beaten by her husband. Her role in the expedition was not as the guide depicted in legend; in fact, she receives scant mention in the Lewis and Clark journals. At one point, when the Corps of Discovery wintered at Fort Clatsop on the Oregon Coast, Sacajawea pleaded to take part in an excursion to see a whale. Lewis wrote, "the Indian woman was very importunate to be permitted to go, and was therefore indulged; she observed she had traveled a long way with us to see the great waters, and that now that monstrous fish was also to be seen, she thought it very hard she could not be permitted to see either." Hardly a guide, Sacajawea had to be granted permission to accompany Lewis to the ocean.

The Lewis and Clark journals document that Sacajawea interpreted for Lewis and Clark at the Shoshoni camp, saved some supplies from washing overboard, and foraged for roots and berries. When Lewis tried to barter with a Chinook for an otter-skin robe, the Chinook would accept nothing but the belt of blue beads Sacajawea wore. She gave up the belt. She served as a *token of peace*, as Clark called her in one notation in his journal. No war party would carry a woman and baby.

One of the most moving parts about Sacajawea in the Lewis and Clark journals describes their arrival at the Shoshoni village where she was born. When Sacajawea saw her brother after many years of separation, she was overcome and could hardly continue to interpret. Sacajawea's heroism did not manifest itself as guide of the Corps of Discovery. Leading the expedition was the genius of Lewis and Clark. It was Sacajawea's resilience and courage that Lewis and Clark commended.

You break the heads of leviathan in pieces
and give him to be meat
to the people of the wilderness.

Psalm 74:14

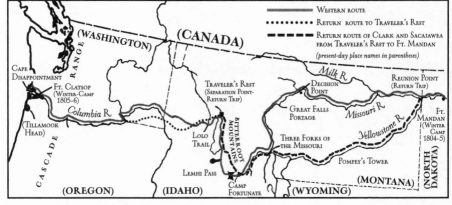

The Lewis and Clark Expedition from Fort Mandan to Fort Clatsop

Excerpt of letter from President Jefferson: "The object of your mission is to explore the Missouri River, and such principle streams of it, as by its course & communication with the waters of the Pacific Ocean, may offer the most direct and practicable water communication across this continent, for the purpose of commerce."

hey hey hey
hey hey hey hey hi

You see horses coming from the sky.
You see them change into canoes and you are rowing.
You see your oars are wings.

You hear the clouds talking.
They talk until they are shouting.
Their voices are hailstones pounding the river.
The water is turbulent and hard to row.
You shake your oars which are wings
but you do not fly.

YOU COME TO the Mandan village with Toussaint Charbonneau and Otter Woman. There is a hunting party heading upriver in the spring. *Explorers*, Toussaint says. They hunt for the headwaters of the Missouri River, for a water route to the Pacific. Toussaint wants to interpret for them.

Otter Woman and you are Shoshoni from the headwaters of the river. You were kidnaped by the Hidatsa. Toussaint bought Otter Woman and you from the Hidatsa. You want to return to the headwaters of the river. You want to return to the Shoshoni.

You see the hailstones again.

The hailstones fall like meteors.
Now the canoes are in the sky.
The canoes change into horses.
You see the horses are ghosts.

[Clark]
4th November Sunday 1804
a fine morning we continued to cut Down trees and raise our houses, a Mr Chaubonie (*Chaboneau*), interpreter for the Gross Ventre nation Came to See us, and informed that he came Down with Several Indians from a hunting expidition up the river, to here [hear] what we had told the Indians in Council this man wished to hire as an interpriter, the wind rose this evening from the East & clouded up. Great numbers of Indians pass hunting and Some on the Return

The Indians call Toussaint *Great Horse from Afar* and *Forest Bear*.
You see the white men do not like him either.
Yet Toussaint wants to go.

You watch the explorers talking to Jessaume, a Frenchman like Toussaint. You see they prefer Jessaume.

The Hidatsa tell explorers there is a Great Falls in the Missouri River. They will need horses to portage the mountains beyond the Falls. They tell them the Shoshoni have horses. They will have to barter with the Shoshoni for the horses.

Toussaint tells the explorers Otter Woman and you are Shoshoni. He tells them you can interpret. He tells them you know the headwaters of the river. Otter Woman and you were taken as girls. They might know you were too young. They might know you don't know the way upriver. But they know you speak Shoshoni. They know you can ask for horses when they need to cross the mountains.

Once you were Shoshoni,
then Hidatsa,
then Charbonneau.
Now you'll speak *horse* in
Shoshoni for the white man.

[Clark]
5 November Monday 1806
I rose verry early and commenced raising the 2 range of
Huts the timber large and heavy
to carry, cotton wood & Elm,
Some ash, Small, our Situation
Sandy, great numbers of Indians
pass to and from hunting a
camp of Mandan

You watch the white men build their fort across the river from the earth lodges of the Mandan village.
When you see their wall, you call it, *place-where-logs-stand-up-side-by-side*.

You hear them call it, *Fort Mandan*.
Already they name the Mandan village theirs. This is how it is done.
With their language they say it is theirs.

That night Otter Woman and you stand under the sky to watch the Northern lights. You have seen them before, but these lights are a spirit you don't know. You tremble with fear, but you do not cry out. Great bears, horses, birds flying, animals stampeding into the sky to get back to the Maker. You feel the baby inside you kick. You hear the moans of the people.

The explorers bring something you don't understand. Yet the sky puts its teepee hide over you.

The old spirits throw their blankets over the next morning. The day is cold and black.

There will be another separation from what you know. You cannot look into the hollows of Otter Woman's eyes.

You know the explorers will change what you are, that you will be taken into them, that they can look past you without thinking.

[Clark]
6th November Tuesday 1804
Fort Mandan
last night late we wer awoke by the Sergeant of the Guard to See a Nothern light, which was light, (but) not red, and appeared to Darken and Some times nearly obscured, and open, (divided about 20 degrees above horizon —various shapes—considerable space) many times appeared in light Streeks, and at other times a great Space light & containing floating collomns which appeared to approach each other & retreat leaveing the lighter space at no time of the Same appearance

This Morning I rose a[t] Day light the Clouds to the North appeared black at 8 oClock the [wind] began to blow hard from the N.W. and Cold, and Continued all Day

[Clark]
11th November Sunday 1804.
Fort Mandan
a cold Day continued to work at the Fort Two men cut themselves with an ax, The large Ducks pass to the South and Indians gave me several roles of parched meat Two Squars of the Rock mountains, purchased from the Indians by a frenchmen came down The Mandan out hunting the Buffalow

You know you are nothing they want. Yet you take them four buffalo robes.

You pull your blanket over your forehead and ears. It's only your feet and hands that are cold. You are going to have a baby and often you feel warm.

Why are they looking for the headwaters? Don't they know the river starts with the Maker? His voice is the headwaters of the Missouri.

Sometimes you see Toussaint looking at his women. What is he deciding? Is he thinking who he will leave behind when the men start upriver? He must not be considering his other wives. He looks at Otter Woman and you. Can't he take both? You don't want to be left behind. Your baby will come before spring. You can carry it with you. You are sure you are going with Otter Woman. You can tell the way Toussaint looks at you. A baby is no more than another burden to carry.

Once you hear something make a sound. You remember when you were a girl and you drove away your cries like birds that would be killed if they were seen.

The explorers ask the Indians the way upriver.
The explorers know there is no continuous river to the place the Indians call *smelly lake*.
But Lewis and Clark don't know how far it is between the rivers.

There are ashes from the fireplace on the plank floor of the captains' quarters.
The Indians draw crooked lines in the ashes to show the explorers the mountains that separate the rivers.

They listen to your voice as you tell them what the Indians say.

The Indians come to watch Lewis and Clark build their fort. It has a front wall with a wide gate. The side walls meet at a point at the back of the fort. Inside the fort, along the two walls, there are six rooms. You like to count them with your fingers.

Toussaint moves you into the fort! Otter Woman and his other wives stay in the Mandan village. It is YOU Toussaint brings and not Otter Woman? Maybe it is these men who allow only one wife.

You and Toussaint are in the room with Jessaume and York, Clark's black man.
The Indians come to look at York. He tells the children he is a bear and growls at them. They laugh and run. You know he has medicine.

The Indians also come to see the large black dog that travels with Captain Lewis.

Already there is ice on the river.

> [Clark]
> 12th December Wednesday 1804–
> a Clear Cold morning Wind from the north The Thermometer at Sun rise Stood 38 below 0

Sometimes water freezes in the cottonwoods and forces them apart. They explode like cannons, making you jump in the night.

Now the river freezes over.

It is so cold, the explorers can't hunt.

They only can stand their watch a short time. Then someone else takes their place until they have to be replaced.

> [Clark]
> 17th December Monday 1804
> a verry Cold morning the Thmt. Stood a[t] 45° below 0

When Toussaint took Otter Woman as a wife, you asked to come with her. You are from the same tribe. The same place. You didn't want to be left with the Hidatsa. You are part of Toussaint's family. You know how to be quiet. You care for the children, carry water, scrape hides, garden, prepare meals. You stay together. There is no other way.

Now Otter Woman sleeps across the frozen river. You talk to her on the edge of the village. Maybe it is just for the winter.

Sometimes at night Toussaint called one of you aside. Other nights you slept beside Otter Woman. Now you sleep beside Toussaint.

Sometimes you dream of the Shoshoni camp. Your parents, brothers and sisters. By yourself you are nothing. You clung to Otter Woman. What good does it do to remember? Why did the Hidatsa take you? To show they could.

Toussaint doesn't know to be quiet. Maybe he was taken from his people too, and his noise keeps him from remembering. Or it keeps him company in a way you can't. How

can a man who sees so little know what to do? Yet he is
the leader of his women and children.

Others have come into the land. First, the French. The
British. Then the Americans. But it was your own Indian
people, not the white men, that took you from your people. You know all men can do the same thing. You know
the meanness of women too. The Hidatsa made you
work. They made you sleep at the coldest edge of the buffalo robe. They gave you the heaviest water to carry.

The Mandan cross the frozen river to Fort Mandan. They
bring corn in exchange for repair of knives and belts.
One man dresses like a woman because a dream told him to.
The explorers look at him but say nothing.

Lewis and Clark have a blacksmith with them.
When the Indians come to the fort, the explorers pass out
small flags and buttons, sometimes knives.

Mostly the explorers are cold.

You know the Indian men hit their women. One woman
cries to get into the fort. Her face is bloody. You hear Lewis
tell the man to take back his wife and not beat her again.

Toussaint tells you, Napoleon Bonaparte sold the land for
fifteen million dollars!
Three cents an acre from Mississippi to the Rocky
Mountains.

What a fool! The British, Spanish, French fight over the land. None of it will belong to any of them. But to the new country, America.

Toussaint tells you, you will lose too. Your land will be lost like his.
You think of someone owning your land, someone far away who has never seen it.
You think of someone selling your land to someone who hasn't seen it either.

Well, here they are: one keelboat, two large pirogues, six dugouts, thirty men, to find out just what Bonaparte sold. To find out what Jefferson bought.

Now the men are on the prairie under open sky. They see the frozen grasslands of the plains with only a few trees.

These two captains, Lewis and Clark. Lewis, the moody one.

It is winter.
The tribes are hungry.
The cold is a spirit that drives you into yourself.

You watch the ritual of *calling buffalo back to the village*.

The old men stand in a circle. The young men go to the old men and request to see their wives who present themselves naked to sleep with the young men all night.

[Clark]
Jan 5th 1805
a Buffalow Dance (or Medeson) (*Medecine*) for 3 nights...

Lewis and Clark don't know what to think.
They look away.
They don't want any women.
Their men do, yes, but not them.

Two days later, the buffalo show up.

Sometimes you remember the Shoshoni running along the edge of the creek in fear, forgetting one another. Your feet were wet. You stumbled. A Hidatsa grabbed you, yanking you from the ground. Your ribs hurt from his grip. He dragged you along the ground, laughed at you because you screamed when you saw the Shoshoni leaving you behind as they fled.

Now you wake in the night feeling your ribs hurt. But it is the baby turning.
It is time, but the baby won't come.

You see the ghost horses. They stand on the edge of the sky. You feel the weight of the baby. Maybe the horses have come to take you.

You speak to the baby. You tell it to come.
The women gather around you. You hear their prayers.

The women come and go
for several nights.

Finally, you feel the baby.

First you have cramps.
Then the pain along your
back and stomach.

[Lewis]
7th February Thursday 1805
This morning was fair Thermometer at 18°, above naught much warmer than it has been for some days; wind S.E. continue to be visited by natives. The Sergt of the guard reported the Indian women (wives to our interpreters) were in the habit of unbaring the fort gate at any time of night and admitting their Indian visitors, I therefore directed a lock to be put to the gate and ordered that no Indian but those attached to the garrison should be permitted to remain all night within the fort or admitted during the period which the gate had been previously ordered to be kept shut, which was from sunset untill sunrise.

You hear the horses stomp their feet. You hear them running at you. You feel their hooves trampling you.

If they stop a moment, you know they will return.
You hear them paw the ground. You hear them snort. You
know the horses are running toward you.
You plead with them.

You beg.
But you feel their feet on
your stomach.
You cannot breathe.

You call Otter Woman.
You call the Maker.

The horses bite you.
Their tails strike.

They are tearing your legs
apart. They are riding your
belly. You feel yourself grow
small. You are nothing beside
a horse. They are running
toward you. They are run-
ning and running. You give
yourself to them. There is
no other way.

The hands of the horses
are upon you. You cry as
they trample.
You hear Otter Woman's
voice. You hear it as medicine.

The horses open their
mouths. They shake you
with their teeth. You snap
like a sapling.

Jessaume is putting some-
thing in your mouth.
It is choking you.

[Lewis]
11th February Monday 1805
The party that were ordered last
evening set out early this morning, the weather was fair and cold
wind N.W. About five Oclock
this evening one of the wives of
Charbono was delivered of a fine
boy. it is worthy of remark that
this was the first child which this
woman had boarn, and as is common in such cases her labour was
tedious and the pain violent; Mr.
Jessome informed me that he
had freequently administered a
small portion of the rattle of the
rattle-snake, which he assured
me had never failed to produce
the desired effect, that of hasten-
ing the birth of the child; having
the rattle of a snake by me I gave
it to him and he administered
two rings of it to the woman
broken in small pieces with the
fingers and added to a small
quantity of water. Whether this
medicine was truly the cause or
not I shall not undertake to
determine, but I was informed
that she had not taken it more
than ten minutes before she
brought forth perhaps this
remedy may be worthy of future
experiments, but I must confess
that I want faith as to it's efficacy.

You want to leave.
There is wind. Hailstones and blizzard.
The land is frozen with pain.

You are a cottonwood. The ice is forcing you apart. You
scream until you split with ice.

Then it is quiet.
Except the sound of a small animal.
It is the baby. Otter Woman wraps him. The women sing
him a song, calling him to this world.

The women lay him on your chest.
Now you are burning with fire. The women fan you. The
baby sneezes. He tries to suck, but you are giving him fire.

You sleep and your dreams are horses. They stand beside
you snorting. They paw the ground. They do not step on
you, but you jump as though they do. You are shivering.
The women are washing you. You jump with the sound of
the water.

They cover you with a buffalo robe.
You see the baby's feet are round as hooves.
You see his horse's eyes.
You sleep and you feel the baby's tail hitting you.

Otter Woman is washing you with snow. You hear her
voice calling you from the fire.
Now you are sweating. You throw off the buffalo robe.

You hear the women's voices.

You look at the planks above you. Why are you in the fort? Toussaint brought you here.
The explorers are going to use Otter Woman and you to ask for horses.
Now you remember you are staying at the fort. But Otter Woman is going on the journey also.

The baby eats.
Then he sleeps.
You see his head is bruised and pushed out of shape.

The women help you up, but your legs buckle and you cannot stand.
Otter Woman stays with you. You sleep holding her hand.

When you wake, Toussaint tells you he named the baby Jean Baptiste Charbonneau.

Now you get up. You stand in the room in the fort.

When you can, you walk to the gate to show the men you will be able to travel in the spring.

Lewis and Clark measure birds and animals. They draw coyotes, prairie wolves, jackrabbits, antelope.
You hear last summer they found a village of small animals that burrowed in the ground, that sat erect and whistled.
They called them barking squirrels. Toussaint calls them *petite chienne*.

You hear the explorers laugh as they tell the story.
You nurse Jean Baptiste as you listen.

The men dug in the holes for the *petite chienne*, they
poured water into the tunnels. They worked all day to
catch the prairie dog.
Now he sits in his pen.

You pet Seaman, Lewis's dog, who watches you feed the
baby.

Lewis and Clark will send boxes and trunks to the city of
Washington in the keelboat: animal skins, bones, the
horns of mountain rams, antlers, bows and arrows, earth-
en pots, Mandan corn, buffalo robes, one robe painted
with a battle fought eight years ago: the Sioux & Ricarars
against the Mandans, Minitarras, and Ahwahharways.

You see the four magpies, the prairie dog, and a prairie
grouse. You hear them cry in their cages. You tell them
they are going on a journey. You tell the magpie maybe it
will sing in the President's house.
You watch the men write in their journals. What do they
say with the gnarl of their letters? How can they say what
the land is like with their marks?

They come to look at the land. But they do not see the
spirits. They write in their journals. But they do not know
the land. They give the animals names which do not
belong to them. Which do not say what they are. Which
do not fit.

They do not hear the birds. They do not see the ghost horses.

The Indians bring a boy to the fort who has been out all night. His feet are frozen. Lewis puts them in cold water.

The boy's toes do not heal. You hear the child scream as Lewis cuts off his toes.

You hear the man yell as Lewis pulls on his dislocated shoulder to get it back into place.

When other children are sick, the Indians bring them to Captain Lewis.
They come to see him with their fevers, boils, tumors, snowblindness, pleurisy, rheumatism, gonorrhea.

Toussaint is angry. He is not in charge. He has found men who are stronger than him. Who can think more than he does. Who can see farther than he does.

Toussaint will not agree to work.
He will not stand guard.
He tells Lewis and Clark, when they start upriver in the spring, he can return from the journey whenever he pleases.
If he gets mad at any man he will turn back.

Toussaint is like one who is snowblind.

He says he will decide how many provisions he will carry.

You say nothing. You know he will hit you.

Lewis and Clark decide not to take Toussaint.
They will leave you behind and they need you to ask for horses.
Toussaint is furious.
He howls like a forest bear.

You give him time to think what he has done.

Your sickness returns and you feel weak. You hide your weakness from the men. You feed the baby in the fort. You and Otter Woman stay to yourselves when she comes from across the river. Sometimes her fingers quiver like the northern lights.

> [Clark]
> 17th of March Sunday
> ...Mr Chabonah Sent a frenchman of our party [to say] he was Sorry for the foolish part he acted and if we pleased he would accompany us agreeabley to the terms we had perposed and doe every thing we wished him to doe &etc. &etc...

The men are talking how to make beads: glass trading beads that are beaten, heated and melted together into larger beads.
You and Otter Woman listen.

Toussaint tells you these men do what Lewis and Clark say. One of them was found resting on his sentinel early in their journey. He received 100 lashes on his bare back.

Another one got drunk. Another talked back to Clark. They also were lashed.

The men should run, Toussaint says.

Where could they run? Swim down river? Walk across the land?
Face the Omahas? The Teton Sioux?

The explorers look for a waterway to the ocean. Do they think they will come to the mountains and roll downhill to the Pacific?

You could tell them, lay on the ground, open one eye, the earth lodges of the Mandan villages are like the mountains they will find.

You haven't been across them. No. But you feel them ahead.

You know they will take you with them. You can tell by their eyes.

You are important to them maybe the way a horse is important to them. You will get them where they want to go.

You hear the explorers say Toussaint can take only *one* of you on the trail.
That's what Toussaint has been deciding.

The young one, then, the one with the baby.

Otter Woman is your friend, your companion. You know Toussaint is going to leave her behind. She has children. She is not able to leave as you are with only one baby. Now you are the one trembling with fear. She holds you under the buffalo robe. It is another parting from what you know. Another tearing away from yourself. Otter Woman tells you not to cry. You have the land, the birds that fly over the land. You will be able to go back to the Shoshoni. The place you are from. Now it is Otter Woman you hear crying. She will be left behind. Without a husband, you know what will happen.

You take your blue beaded belt. You pack white weasel tails from the weasels you trapped. You leave upriver with Lewis and Clark and the men in their pirogues and canoes.

You do not look back.

The keelboat with its boxes, trunks, animals, and *specimens* is sent back downriver. Two of the white men, Newman and Reed, go with it because of their insubordination.

You sing to the baby. They call you *Bird Woman*. The strands of your hair move like feathers, they say. They row up river and you row with them. When the baby cries you feed him. You watch the shore go by as the men row upriver. When the baby is asleep, you row.

[Clark]
Fort Mandan April th 7th 1805 Sunday, at 4 oClock PM, the Boat... Set out down the river for St Louis. at the same time we Sout out on our voyage up the river in 2 perogues and 6 canoes, and proceded on to the 1st villag. Of Mandan & camped on S.S. our party consisting of Sergt Nathaniel Pryor Sgt John Ordway. Sgt Pat. Gass; William Bratten, John Colter Joseph & Reubin Fields, John Shields, George Gibson, George Shannon, John Potts, John Collins, Jos. Whitehouse, Richard Windser, Alexander Willard, Hugh Hall, Silas Gutrich, Robert Frazuer, Peter Crouzat, John Baptiest la page, Francis Labich, Hue McNeal, William Warner, Thomas P. Howard, Peter Wiser, John B. Thompson, and my black servent york, George Drew yer who acts as hunter & interpreter, Shabonah and his *Indian Squar* to act as Interpreter & interpretress for the snake Indians—one Mandan & Shabonahs infant. *Sah-kah-gar we a*

Sometimes you cannot proceed upriver.
The wind blows sand into your face. You stay in your tents with the men. You cover the baby's face as he nurses. You cover your own face in the blowing dust.

It is dust from the feet of the ghost horses.
Sometimes you know they are stirring the land. There is a change you do not want, but there is nothing you can do.

You hear the voices of the plants as you walk. You know where they are. You know what they say.
You remember how your mother and grandmother taught you to listen.

You dig roots for the men.

Sometimes you cramp. The ache in your stomach does not go away.

[Lewis]
Tuesdsay April 9th
...the squaw busied herself in serching for the wild artichokes which the mice collect and deposit in large hoards. this operation she performed by penetrating the earth with a sharp stick about some small collection of drift wood. her labour soon proved successful, and she procured a good quantity of these roots...

You walk behind the men anyway.

Jean Baptiste is a bird nest on your back.
A pouch of buffalo meat.

Sometimes you walk on the shore with Toussaint and Clark.
Other times you sit in the boat all day.
You row.
You feed the baby.

At night, you find a branch for a brace against your back.

You hear Lewis and Clark ask why they see no other Indians. It's because the word has been passed. Or it's because it's the time they are someplace else.

Before Lewis and Clark arrived at the Mandan village, the Teton Sioux held the cord of one of their boats. The explorers drew swords and uncovered the cannon and said it was *Bad Medicine.*
Let go of the canoe.
Black Buffalo intervened and said the women and children only wanted to see the keel boat, the pirogues and canoes. They were given a tour and Lewis and Clark pushed on.

The Indians know these men aren't afraid.

You watch the land as you row upriver. You tell the land to hide itself, to run from the shore like the herd of deer you see.

The canoe moves forward when the men pull back on the oars, then slows when they take the oars from the water to pull back again. The movement rocks Jean Baptiste. You watch him sleep as you row.

[Clark]
18th April Thursday 1805
...one Beaver and a Musrat cought this morning, the beaver cought in two traps, which like to have brought about a misunderstanding between two of the party &c. after brackfast I assended a hill and observed that the river made a great bend to the South, I concluded to walk thro' the point about 2 miles and take Shabono, with me, he had taken a dost of Salts &c his squar followed on with her child, when I struck the next bend of the [river] I left this man & his wife & child on the river bank and went out to hunt, Killed a young Buck Elk, & a Deer, the Elk was tolerable meat, the Deer verry pore...

Some mornings there is still ice on the oars. Lewis's large dog, Seaman, is lost, but he returns the next day. There are bears that eat dogs, you tell Seaman. The Indians eat dogs too.

He looks at you, but does not hear.

He kills a small antelope.

[Clark]
19th of April Friday 1805
a blustering windey day...

Now Seaman chases a beaver. He thinks he can catch anything. The beaver turns on him. It bites him so bad, he limps. He cries and stays close to Lewis when they walk.

You want to cry also because you ache, but you keep walking.

[Clark]
30th of April Tuesday 1805
I walked on Shore to day our interpreter & his squar followed, in my walk the squar found & brought me a bush something like the currunt, which she said bore delicious froot and that great quantitis grew on the Rocky Mountains... I saw Great numbers of antelopes, also scattering Buffalow, Elk, Deer, wolves, Gees, ducks & Crows. I Killed 2 Gees which we dined on to day...

They call you *Bird Woman* as if you flew over the trail above them, but you walk behind them. You listen to their voices. You see the new men that have come to your land. Now the Hidatsa can be taken. Now they can be defeated. Now they will know what it's like. Maybe the white man will take their daughters, grabbing them by the arm, gripping them by the chest, cracking their ribs like a small bundle of twigs.

You hear the hooves of their horses on the rocks. But they don't hear. You hear the pecking of a rock against a teepee stake. *Clack. Clack.* You know they don't hear.

You watch the white men write. You see they number their days in their journal.

Toussaint drinks with them. You see the barrels of food they bring: apples, dried fruit. They hunt for meat and fish, berries and roots.

A song comes to you, but you do not sing it for them.
You know the song has medicine.
You know it has the power of the clouds talking.

The men spend their days lifting the pirogues and canoes from sawyers and sandbars. They pole and pull their boats upriver. The wind is cold against the rolling, short-grass prairie. When it comes from behind, the men can use the sails. But mostly, they push against the current.

[Lewis]
Thursday May 2nd 1805
...every thing which is incom-prehensible to the indians they call *big medicine*, and is the opperation of the presnts [presence] and power of the *great sperit*. this morning one of the men shot the indian dog that followed us for several days, he would stalk their cooked provisions.

You pass the river-that-scolds-all-others.

The land is wide. Beyond the river, the trees are sparse. The hills are in the distance.

The men come to talk to Jean Baptiste. They watch him sleep.

Sometimes you are tired. But you keep walking.

The men hunt elk and black-tailed mule-deer for skins.

You clean and string the elk hooves.
You make them rattle for Jean Baptiste.

Lewis writes, *pitch pine, Dwarf cedar, scattering pines.*

If you could write, you would say, *early in the morning, the spirits are still on the earth.*

Thursday May 9th 1805
...Capt C. killed 2 bucks and 2 buffaloe... we saved the best of the meat... for making what our wrighthand cook Charbono calls the *boudin (poudingue) blanc*... a white pudding one of the del[ic]acies of the forrest... About 6 feet of the large gut of the Buffaloe... he holds fast at one end with the right hand, while with the forefinger and thumb of the left he compresses it and discharges what he says *is not good to eat*... the mustle under the shoulder blade next to the back, and the fillets are... needed up with kidney suit [suet]... salt pepper flour... it is then baptised in the missouri... and bobbed into a kettle... and fryed with bears oil untill it becomes brown.

The buffalo and elk follow you sometimes.
The men throw stones at them
to make them go away.

Sometimes they are buffalo calves who have lost their mothers. They will not live long.

You feel like one of them. You walk without-those-you-know, without-those-you-belong-to. But for Jean Baptiste, you feel like an empty earth lodge.

You cross muddy, slippery ground. The men have stone bruises and infection from the thorns of the prickly pear on their feet. The men make new moccasins from hides and try to repair old ones.

You see rattlesnakes and grizzlies.
Sometimes the grizzlies come after the men.
The men fire again and again into one grizzly before it dies.

Lewis kills some birds and spends all evening looking at them. He measures them, thinks about them, makes notes and drawings of them. He turns them over, makes more observations, and more notes.

Sometimes he writes wavy lines on his paper for the river and its tributaries.
Toussaint tells you not to watch him.
But you want to see this new vision quest.

[Lewis]
Thursday May 9th 1805
I killed four plover this evening of a different species from any I have yet seen... it is about the size of the yellow legged or large grey plover common to the lower part of this river... the eye is moderately large, are black with a narrow ring of dark yellowish brown; the head, neck, upper part of the body and coverts of the wings are a dove coloured brown, which when the bird is at rest is the predominant colour; the breast and belley are of a brownish white; the tail is composed of 12 feathers of 3 Ins. being of equal length, of those the two in the center are black, with traverse bars of yellowish brown; the others are a brownish white. the large feathers of the wings are white tiped with blacked. The beak is black, 2 1/2 inches in length, slightly tapering, streight, of a cilindric form and blontly or roundly pointed; the chaps are of equal length, and nostrils narrow, longitudinal and connected; the feet and legs are smooth and of a greenish brown; has three long toes and a sho[r]t one on each foot, the long toes are unconnected with a web, and the short one is placed very high up the leg

The pirogue is at full sail when a squall hits the river. You remember your vision of horses. You don't see them, but you think the horses shake the sail in their mouths. You fear the pirogue will turn over in the waves.

Toussaint looses his head. He lets go of the rudder. *Mon Dieu*, he cries. The boat tips. You see the instruments start to fall. You grab them. And the journals. While you hold the baby.

Lewis and Clark are standing on shore. They see the boat on its side. They yell at Toussaint. They fire their rifles. You are still fishing their cases of instruments from the river.

Cruzatte, in the bow of the boat, threatens to shoot Toussaint if he doesn't get hold of the rudder and try to right the boat. Cruzatte orders the men to haul in the sail. Slowly the boat is righted. Then Cruzatte orders the men to bail water.

behind, insomuch that is dose not touch the ground when the bird stands erect. the notes of this bird are louder and more various than any other of this family that I have seen.

[Lewis]
Tuesday May 14th 1805
a suddon squall of wind struck us and turned the perogue so much on the side as to allarm Sharbono who was steering at the time, in this state of alarm he threw the perogue with her side to the wind, when the spritsail gibing was as near oversetting the perogue as it was possible to have missed. the wind however abating for an instant I ordered Drewyer to the helm and the sails to be taken in, which was instant[ly] executed and the perogue being steered before the wind was agin plased in a state of security. this accedent was very near costing us dearly. Believing this vessell to be the most steady and safe, we had embarked on board of it our instruments, Papers, medicine and the most valuable part of the merchandize which we had still in reserve as presents for the Indians. We had also embarked on board ourselves, with three men who could not swim and the squaw with the

young child, all of whom, had the perogue overset, would most probably have perished, as the waves were high, and the perogue upwards of 200 yards from the nearest shore; however we fortunately escaped and pursued our journey under the square sail, which shortly after the accident I directed to be again hoisted...

On shore, Lewis and Clark look through their supplies they cannot get along without: medicines, books, clothing, cases of instruments: quadrant, protractor, sextant, chronometer, microscope, magnet, compasses, knives, axes, spontoons. You listen to their words as they take inventory: canisters of powder, rifles, pistols, flintlock muskets, blunderbusses, the swivel canon, the fiddles, whiskey...

They name the next tributary *Bird Woman River*.

The men call Jean Baptiste *Pompey*. You are not sure what that means, but they tell you he was a warrior in another land. You hear the men say his name, *Pomp. Pomp.*

You feed the baby. The men play with him.
Why did Toussaint come on the journey? For France? His parents left their land. They settled in Canada. No. Toussaint comes to see what animals there are upriver. Maybe he is thinking of getting back to the Canadian Fur Company. Maybe he wants the Northwest Fur Company. Toussaint hits you when they are not looking because the men want to stop and talk to Pomp and you.
You are Toussaint's. Jean Baptiste is Toussaint's. *Pomp. Pomp.* They call the baby.

Bonaparte sold the land!
He tells you the Indians are sold too.
Your husband is angry the French lost the land. The French
were first! Napolean sells the country to America? Now they
have everything but the Spanish and Oregon Territory.

Toussaint is stuck with his
wife on his hands. He
shows the other men he is
not burdened with you.

Mon Dieu.

You hear the men talk.
Someone says to Toussaint,
by selling the land, Bonaparte gives England a rival:
the new country, America.
You see Toussaint has not
thought of that.

How can they put a new
nation over yours?
How can they just come
and announce it *theirs*?

Lewis and Clark find an
Indian camp. They show
you the moccasins they find.
You tell them they are not
of the Shoshoni (Snake)
nation, but of the Indians
who inhabit the country on
this side of the Rocky
Mountains and north of
the river.

[Lewis]
Wednesday May 29th 1805
Last night we were all allarmed
by a large buffaloe Bull, which
swam over from the opposite
shore and coming along side of
the white perogue, climbed over
it to land, he then allarmed ran
up the bank in full speed directly
towards the fires, and was within
18 inches of the heads of some of
the men who lay sleeping before
the centinel could allarm him or
make him change his course, still
more alarmed, now he took his
direction immediatley towards
our lodge, passing between 4
fires and within a few inches of
the heads of one range of the
men as they yet lay sleeping,
when he came near the tent, my
dog saved us by causing him to
change his course a second time,
which he did by turning a little
to the right, and was quickly
out of sight, leaving us by this
time in an uproar with our guns
in o[u]r hands, enquiring of each
other the ca[u]se of the alarm,
which after a few moments was
explained by the centinel: we
were happy to find no one hirt...

They say they haven't seen Indians since Fort Mandan, but their hunting camps are here. You see their prayer cloth offerings, their sweat lodge frames, teepee rings, fire pits, horse tracks. You know the Indians stay out of sight.

You come to the white cliffs of the Missouri Breaks. The explorers say the sandstone cliffs have been carved into ghost shapes by the wind.
But you think it is the place where the ghost horses cross the river. The cliffs are shaped by the hooves of their feet where they climb.

The elk tow-rope snaps on the white pirogue and nearly capsizes it again.
Lewis says the white pirogue is attended by some evil spirit.

In the evening, you walk by the river holding Jean Baptiste. It is here you find a white stone in the shape of a beaver.

When you were born, you had light skin. Your grand-mother dreamed of a small, white beaver without a tail. It had a stone heart because it had a long journey to walk. A tail and a soft heart would slow it. When the beaver cried, your grandmother saw it had short, dull teeth. It would not build a dam. It would not slam the water with its tail. It would not cut down trees. But it would walk on a long journey. It would know places the Shoshoni had not known.

You dream of your grandmother in the night. Your bed is wet from rain and you are cold.

The next day you hear the shots from the canoe. One after another.

Later Toussaint tells you he was almost killed by a bear as the men hunted.

[Lewis]
Sunday June 2nd 1805.
The wind blew violently last night and was attended by a light shower of rain; the morning fair and we set out at an early hour... Accordingly I walked on shore most of the day with some of the hunters... killed 6 Elk 2 buffal[o]e 2 Mule deer and a bear... the bear was very near catching Drewyer; it also pursued Charbono who fired his gun in the air as he ran but fortunately eluded the vigilence of the bear by secreting himself very securely in the bushes untill Drewyer finally killed it by a shot in the head; the (only) shot indeed that will conquer the farocity of those tremendious anamals...

At night you feel your sickness. You shiver and sweat.

Lewis and Clark camp at a fork in the river they call Decision Point because they can't decide which way to take. The men say the north fork; Lewis and Clark say the south.

You do not know which way they should take.

Lewis decides to scout the north fork first.

While you are camped at the fork of the two rivers, you feel your weakness. You ask the Maker to let you walk.

What you need is a rest. Your legs tremble. You shift the baby on your back. He is a rock you carry. He is the moon on your back.

[Lewis]
Monday June 3rd 1805
This morning early we passed over and formed a camp on the point formed by the junction of two large rivers... An interesting question was now to be determined; which of these rivers was the Missouri, or that river which the Minnetares call *Amahte Arzzha* or Missouri... to mistake the stream at this period of the season, two months of the traveling season having now elapsed, and to ascend such stream to the rocky Mountain or perhaps much further before we could inform ourselves whether it did approach the Columbia or not, and then be obliged to return that take the other stream would not only loose us the whole of this season but would probably dishearted the party that it might defeat the expedition altogether... accordingly we dispatched two light canoes with three men in each up those steams; we also sent out several small parties by land with instructions to penetrate the country as far as they conveniently can permitting themselves time to retun this evening...

The men are at a fork in the river. The muddy fork comes from the north. The clear fork comes from the southwest. You hear the men talk. The Indians did not tell them about this large fork. Lewis and Clark think the Missouri is the clear fork. The rest of the men say it is the muddy one. You feed the baby as they camp. You bend over in pain. You feel the cramps in your stomach. You shiver. Toussaint gives you another buffalo robe. You cover your head. When the baby sleeps you let yourself sleep also. You hear the men's voices. They don't know where they are. You feel the fork of two rivers. You feel the two worlds coming together. You are sweating. You are cold. The pain rocks you. When you sleep the river hisses. The men's voices cut your ears. They give you medicine to drink. You only want to hear Otter Woman. They tell you she is not there. They cut into your arm. The white men settle any disease by letting blood. You enter the earth like a stream. You feel the current of the delirium. You see your dreams while you wake. You feel Otter Woman hold your hand.

You feel the wavy lines.
You are sick.
Clark bleeds your arm again.
He gives you a dose of salts which make you worse. You have pain that does not stop. Clark gives you bark, laying it on your stomach.

The ghost horses are walking on the river. You think of walking with the horses. You could leave your sickness and follow them.

You remember the buffalo calves that followed you. They had lost their mothers and would be eaten by the wolves. You tell Jean Baptiste he will not be like them.

A little buffalo calf licks your arm from the other world.

You tell the ghost horses to leave. They are nothing you can ride. They do not pull a travois.

You see small beings. You call them animal spirits. Half animal, half spirit. Buffalo, elk, bear, no larger than a prairie dog.
You watch them like you see Lewis watch the animals.
The buffalo has stars on its hind legs.
The elk has small spots on its back as if moons.
The black bear has hailstones for eyes. When it growls, white sparks fly from its mouth like snow.
Now you see smaller animal beings.
A badger with blue spots and a small lightning bolt for a tail.
A porcupine with a cloud riding its back. Its teeth pull your sleeve. But you know it is the baby they hold to your breast.

You see the white beaver without a tail. Your remember your grandmother's dream. How she gave you a white stone in the shape of a beaver without its tail.

[Clark]
June 10th Monday 1805
a fine day dry all our articles
arrange our baggage burry
some Powder & lead in the
point, Some Lead a canister of
Powder & an ax in a thicket in
the point at some distance, and
in the large cache or hole we
buried on the up land near the
S. fork 1 mile up S.S. We drew
up our large Perogue into the
middle of a small Island in the
North fork and covered her
with bushes after makeing her
fast to the trees, branded several trees to prevent the Indians
injureing her, at 3 oClock we
had hard wind from the S.W.
thunder and rain for about an
hour after which we repaired &
corked the canoes & loaded
them. Sahcahgagwea our Indian
woman verry sick I blead her,
we deturmined to assend the
South fork, and one of us, Capt
Lewis or my self to go by land
as far as the Snow mountains S.
20°. W. and examine the river
& countrey course &c be cer-
tain of our assending the proper river...

When you are sick you hear
voices from the next world.
You hear their rattles and
drums.

They say they come to
help you.

[Clark]
June 11th Tuesday 1805
...the Indian woman verry sick,
I blead her which appeared to
be of great service to her, both
rivers riseing fast...

When you sleep
the animal beings nuzzle you.
But you see it is Clark.
He wants you to live.
The explorers want you to ask the Shoshoni for horses.
Now there is some connection to them.
These-men-that-take.
You walk as one of them.

[Clark]
June 12th 1805 Wednesday
last night was clear and cold,
this morning fair we set out at
8 oClock & proceeded on
verry well wind from the S.W.
The enterpreters wife verry
sick so much so that I move her
into the back part of the covered part of the Perogue which
is cool, her own situation being
a verry hot one in the bottom
of the Perogue, exposed to the
Sun. Saw emence No of swallows in the 1st bluff on the
Lard Side, water very swift, the
bluff are blackish clay & coal
for about 80 feet...

You see the spirits hover-
ing over you.
Do they want you to ask
for ghost horses?

You see you are bigger
than the buffalo, the elk,
the bear.

But the ghost horses are
bigger than you.

You remember the explorers have not found the Great Falls.

You wonder if the expedition will stall.

Maybe Lewis will get lost as he searches for the Falls.

You feel your weakness.

You slip into a dream again.

You wonder if you will make the rest of the journey.

[Clark]
June 13th Thursday 1805
a fair morning, some dew this morning the Indian woman verry sick I gave her a doste of salts... goose berries are ripe and in great abundance, the yellow current is also common, not yet ripe... the Indian woman verry sick. Killed a goat & f raser 2 Buffalow

[Lewis]
Thursday June 13th 1805
...I sent Feels on my right and Drewyer and Gibson on my left with orders to kill some meat and join me at the river where I should halt for dinner. I had proceded on this course about two miles with Goodrich at some distance behind me whin my ears were saluted with the agreeable sound of a fall of water and advancing a little further I saw the spray arrise above the plain like a collumn of smoke... I determined to fix my camp for the present and dispatch a man in the morning to inform Capt C. and the party of my success in finding the falls and settle in their minds all further doubts as to the Missouri...

[Clark]
June 14th Friday 1805
a fine morning the Indian woman complaining all night & excessively bad this morning. her case somewhat dangerous. two men with the Tooth ake 2 with Tumers, & one man with a Tumor & a slight fever passed the camp Capt Lewis made the 1st night at which place he had left part of two bear their skins &c...

You hear Jean Baptiste cry. His voice sounds like water.

The ghost horses are
explorers from the sky.
They have wooden boats
and oars that shoot cannons.
They fill the land with
birds.
They pull the river for-
ward with their oars.

Toussaint leans over you.
He tells you Captain Lewis
has sent a messenger.
He tell you Lewis has
found the Falls and you are
moving toward them.

[Clark]
June the 15th Satturday 1805
a fair morning and worm, we set
out at the usial time and proceeded on with great dificuelty as
the river is more rapid we can
hear the falls this morning verry
distinctly. Our Indian woman
sick & low spirited I gave her the
bark & apply it externely to her
region which revived her much.
The current excessively rapid
and dificuelt to assend great
numbers of dangerous places,
and the fatigue which we have to
encounter is incretiatable The
men in the water from morning
untill night hauling the cord &
boats walking on sharp rocks and
round slipery stones which alter-
nately cut their feet & throw
them down... aded to those difi-
cuelties the rattle snakes [are]
inumerable & require great cau-
tion to prevent being bitten... we
passed a white clay which mixes
with water like flour in every
respect, the Indian woman much
wors this evening, she will not
take any medison, her husband
petetions to return &c, river
more rapid late in the evening we
arrived at a rapid which appeared
so bad that I did not think it prudent to attempt passing of it this
evening as it was not late, we saw
great numbers of Gees Ducks,
crows Blackbirds &c.

You feel a shadow over you. You think it is a spirit animal, and you are afraid, but you see it is Lewis's dog, Seaman, who stands beside you.

[Lewis]
Sunday June 16th 1805.
...about 2 P.M. I reached camp and found the Indian woman extreemly ill and much reduced by her indisposition. This gave me some concern as well for the poor object herself, then with a young child in her arms, as from the consideration of her being our only dependence for a friendly negociation with the Snake Indians on whom we depend for horses to assist us in our portage from the Missouri to the columbia river... I found that two doses of barks and opium which I had given her since my arrival had produced an alteration in her pulse for the better; they were now much fuller and more regular. I caused her to drink the mineral water altogether. w[h]en I first came down I found that her pulse were scarcely perceptible, very quick frequently irregular and attended with strong nervous symptoms, that of the twitching of the fingers and leaders of the arm; now the pulse had become regular much fuller and a gentle perspiration had taken place; the nervous systoms have also in great measure abated, and she feels herself much freer from pain. she complains principally of the lower region of the abdomen, I therefore continued the cataplasms of barks and laudnumn which had been previously used by my friend Capt. Clark. I believe her disorder originated principally from an obstruction of the mensis in consequence of taking could [cold]...

The next morning you ask for food. They give you broiled buffalo and some meat soup.
Lewis adds his medicine.

[Clark]
June 16th of Sunday 1805
Some rain last night a cloudy morning wind hard from the S.W. we set our passed the rapid by double manning the Perogue and coanes and halted at 1/4 of a mile to examine the rapids above... the Indian woman very bad, & will take no medisin what ever, untill her husband finding her out of her sences, easyly provailed on her to take medison, if she dies it will be the fault of her husband I am now convinced. we crossed the river [the] after part of the day and formed a camp from which we intended to make the first portage, Capt Lewis stayed on the Std Side to direct the canoes over the first riffle 4 of them passed this evening the other unloaded & part of the Perogue Loading taken out...

You know you will get up and walk.
The baby is a medicine bundle on your back.
You remember the white stone beaver.
You remember its stone heart.

Lewis]
Monday June 17th 1805
...The Indian woman much better today; I have still continued the same course of medecine; she is free from pain clear of fever, her pulse regular, and eats as heartily as I am willing to permit her of broiled buffaloe well seasoned with pepper and salt and rich soope of the same meat; I think therefore that there is every rational hope of her recovery...

[Lewis]
Tuesday June 18th 1805.
...The Indian woman is recovering fast she set up the greater part of the day and walked out for the fi[r]st time since she arrived here; she eats hartily and is free from fever or pain. I continue same course of medecine and regimen expect that I added one doze of 15 drops of the oil of vitriol today about noon...

When you can, you get up to show the men you can.

In the early morning, the breath of horses rises from the river.
You feed Jean Baptiste while the men sleep. You see the Maker at the river. He leans down to drink.
He is the-one-who-is-with-you. No, the-one-you-are-with.

The earth is a presence.
A place that has breath.

The fog drifts away into the sun.
You know you are the river.
The trees.
The air.

Toussaint, ordered to watch you, lets you eat white apples and dried fish. Your pain returns.
You hear Lewis angry at Toussaint.
Lewis gives you medicine again.

Afterwards, you recover.

[Lewis]
Wednesday, June 19th 1805
This morning I sent out several men for the meat which was killed yesterday, a few hours after they returned with it, the wolves had not discovered it. I also dispatched George Drewyer Reubin Fields and George Shannon on the North side of the Missouri with orders to proceed to the entrance of Medecine river and indeavour to kill some Elk... The wind blew violently the greater part of the day... the Indian woman was much better this morning she walked out and gathered... white apples of which she ate so heartily in their raw state, together with a considerable quantity of dryed fish without my knowledge that she complained very much and her fever again returned. I rebuked Sharbono severely for suffering her to indulge herself with such food he being privy to it and having been previously told what she must only eat. I now gave her broken doses of diltued nitre [saltpeter] untill it produced perspiration and at 10 pm 30 drops of laudnumm which gave her a tolerable nights rest. I amused myself in fishing several hours today and caught a number of both species of the white fish, but no trout nor Cat. I employed the men in making up our baggage in proper packages for transporation...

As you travel

Lewis names the tributaries after his men. There is even a York's Dry Fork.

At one place, a dead tree caught fire and burned a tent. He named it, Burnt Lodge Creek.

He names:

Teapot.

Big Dry Creek.

Butter Island.

No Preserves Island (where the expedition ran out of preserves).

Onion Island.

Rollijay (a name given to Lewis in a dream, he says).

Slaughter River (where wolves eat drowned buffalo) (the stink of which drives us on).

One river Clark calls Judith, the woman he wants to marry. At Decision Point, where the explorers decided which fork to take, Lewis named the north fork Maria's River (a cousin or someone he thought he would marry).

Even Lewis's dog has a name. *Seaman*. An animal with a man's name!

Toussaint says the dog is from Newfoundland, a place by the eastern sea. The dog is a sea man. You laugh thinking of Seaman in the middle of the plains.

This sea of grass.

Seaman barks all night because a bear eats the buffalo suet.

He also barks when no bears are near.

Seaman, *the squirrel-chaser*, the men tease him.

The men plaster themselves with bear grease against the mosquitos.

If you had another name, it would be woman-with-the-stone-beaver's-heart.

You hear a noise in the distance.

You hear the ghost horses running. They click their hooves against the rocks that sound like guns. They come to war. They come to fight.

The birds beat their iron wings.

Otter Woman clacks her iron teeth.

The Maker is charging the world.

When you hear the noise, you are afraid you are getting sick again, but you know the noise is from the land, and not the other world.

[Clark]
June 20th Thursday 1805
Duering the time of my being on the Plains and above the falls I as also all my party repeatedly heard a nois which proceeded from a Direction a little to the N. of West, a loud [noise] and resembling precisely the discharge of a piece of ordinance of 6 pounds at the distance of 5 or six miles. I was informed of it several times by the men J. Fields particularly before I paid any attention to it, thinking it was thunder most probably which they had mistaken. at length walking in the plains yesterday near the most extreem S. E bend of the River above the falls I heard this nois very distinctly, it was perfectly calm clear and not a cloud to be seen, I halted and listened attentively about two hour[s] dureing which time I heard two other discharges, and took the direction of the sound with my pocket

You remember Lewis called his cannon *Bad Medicine*. But it is the sickness they bring with their power.

compass which was a nearly West from me as I could estimate the sound. I have no doubt but if I had leasure I could find from whence it issued. I have thought it probable that it might be caused by running water in some of the caverns of those emence mountains, on the principle of the blowing caverns; but in such case the sounds would be periodical and regular, which is not the case with this, being sometimes heard once only and at other times several dischages in quick successions. it is heard also at different times of the day and night... I well recollect hereing the Miniatarees say that those Rocky mountains made a great noise, but they could not tell me the cause, neither could they inform me of any remakable substance of situation in these mountains which would autherise a conjecture of a probable cause... noise...

Now there is another noise. You are approaching the Great Falls in the Missouri River.

You see why it is the called the *Great Falls*. It is a series of waterfalls which cannot be crossed in boats. The explorers will portage around the Falls.

They make camp to prepare. They do not complain or speak of their hardship. They unload the boats; they make rollers for the boats. They look up the steep hill. They climb.

Day after day they portage the four falls of the Great Falls. They make more truck frames of cottonwood onto which they place wheels. They pull or carry the pirogues, canoes, dugouts and supplies 18 miles over the hills by the falls.

[Clark]
June 22nd Satturday 1805
a fine morning Capt Lewis my self and all the party except a Serjeant Ordway Guterich and the Interpreter and his wife Sac-car-gah-we-a (who are left at camp to take care of the baggage left) across the portage with one canoe on truck wheels and loaded with part of our baggage... we got within half a mile of our intended camp much fatigued at dark, our tongus broke & we took a load to the river on the mens back, where we found a number of wolves which had destroyed a great part of our meat...

You carry Jean Baptiste on your back. The men carry the boats on their back.
You see them strain under the weight of the boats.
You see the ropes cut into their shoulders as they pull.
You see their feet step on sharp rocks and prickly pears.

You look into the falls: the place-where-the-ghost-horses-dance.

Now you wait while a large herd of buffalo cross the river. *10,000*, Clark says. You swat mosquitos and eye gnats. You pull the thorns of the prickly pear from your feet. You suffer violent weather and sudden storms which make the runoff channels slick with clay. Another bear chases the men. It takes several of them shooting to kill it. The islands are *infested with grisleys*, Clark says.

[Lewis]
Monday June 24th 1805
...The Indian woman is now perfectly recovered...

[Lewis]
Tuesday June 25th 1805.
Capt Clark somewhat unwell today. He made Charbono kook for the party against their return. it is worthy of remark that the winds are sometimes so strong in these plains that the men informed me that they hoisted a sail in the canoe and it had driven her along on the truck wheels...

[Clark]
June 26th Wednesday 1805
...& set Chabonah to trying up the Buffalo tallow & put into the empty Kegs &c
I assorted our articles for to be left at this place buried... Cattrages a few small lumbersom articles Capt Lewis Desk and some books & small articles in it...

Now there is rain and hail
like running herds.
You have no place to turn.
The baby is in his little
pouch.
You take him from your
back.
You hide in the rock.

The bier in which you
carry John Baptiste is
swept away at your feet
and you only have time to
grab the baby. He is cold
and you are wet and cold.

York searches for the men
and you.
You follow him back to
camp.

Other men return to camp
mauled with hailstones
that knocked them down.
They are naked.
Bloody.

[Lewis]
Saturday June 29th 1805
...Transaction and occurrencies
which took place with Capt
Clark and party today... he took
with him his black man York,
Sharbono and his indian woman
on his arrival at the falls he
perceived a very black cloud
rising in the West which
threatened immediate rain; he
looked about for a shelter but
could fine none without being
in great danger of being blown
into the river should the wind
prove as violent as it sometimes
is on... the plains; at length he
discovered a rivene where
there were some shelving rocks
under which he took shelter
near the river with Sharbono
and the Indian woman; laying
guns, compass &c. under a
shelving rock on the upper side
of the rivene where they were
perfectly secure from the rain...
soon after a most violent tor-
rent of rain decended accompanied with hail; the rain...
instantly collected in the rivene
and came down in a rolling tor-
rent with irrisistable force driv-
ing rocks mud and everything
before it... Capt Clark seized
his gun and shot pouch with
his left hand with the right
assisted himself up the steep
bluff shoving occasionally the

You hear Clark telling Lewis what they lost:
large compas
an elegant fusee
Tomahawk
Humbrallo
shot pouch & horn with pow-
der & Ball
Mockersons
& the woman lost her childs
Bear [the rawhide shoulder-
pack in which the child rides]
& Clothes bedding &c

You like their lists. You like their numbers.

bluff shoving occasionally the Indian woman before him who had her child in her arms; Sharbono had the woman by the hand indeavouring to pull her up the hill but was so much frightened that he remained frequently motionless and but for Capt C both himself and his [wo]man and child must have perished... So sudden was the rise of the water that before Capt C could reach his gun and begin to ascend the bank it was up to his waist and wet his watch... one moment longer & it would have swept them into the river just above the great cataract...

You see the iron frame for a boat Lewis has carried with him. He says, when covered with skins, it is light enough for two or three men to carry, yet in the water, it can carry hundreds of pounds of supplies.

The men hunt for elk and buffalo skins to cover the iron frame. You hear Lewis talk about the boat he has invented. The men calk the boat with buffalo tallow, beeswax and pounded charcoal. As soon as it is in the river, it leaks and begins to sink.

You see Lewis realize his iron-frame boat will not carry supplies. It will not even float.

You see the sadness of his idea that has to be left behind. You want to say it is Otter Woman to him.

Lewis says maybe it was the lack of proper gum.
You say, in Shoshoni, maybe it doesn't fit the-way-the-wind-that-moves.

You see Lewis sink with his boat.

Two new dugouts have to be made.

But he will continue upriver from the Great Falls.

Eight vessels set out carrying men, baggage and dried meat.
The river is confined to a narrow channel.
The river crooked.
The bottom narrow.
The cliffs high and steep.
The mosquitos troublesome.

There is one-you-talk-to-as-yourself. There is one-who-is-the-same-as-you. Otter Woman. The other women.
You are without them as you row and walk and camp with the men. Jean Baptiste does not know what it is to hear the voices of the women and children. How will he know to-be-with-others-of-himself?

You talk to Jean Baptiste. You tell him of the *lone man* who made an ark to save the Mandan when a flood covered the earth. Jean Baptiste looks at you with his black eyes that are two little fish moving together. You try to make for him all the voices of the village. You speak-as-one-with-the-wind-and-the-birds. You miss the smell of the earth lodge, the hides, the fire pit, the tobacco. You make the voices for yourself also.

You look at these explorers, these white men away from their villages. Yet they move together as a village. You are one of them. They are the other voices for Jean Baptiste. They are the other voices for you. But there is an away-from-them. It is an earth lodge you feel in your chest.

Sometimes the explorers split up. Lewis goes one way. Clark another. They decide on a place to meet. They will discharge guns to find one another. Or leave notes in a tree. It is here that Clark takes an Indian road over a mountain.

You camp on a clear run of cold water.
You poke in the currants and chokecherry.
You build a small fire. The smoke keeps mosquitos from biting Jean Baptiste.
You feed him pieces of suet dumplings with your milk.
You clean his bottom at the river.

You see mountain rams on the face of cliff, walking on their narrow ledges where the wolves and bears cannot get them. You point to them for Jean Baptiste.

Lewis kills two elk. You chew a piece of meat no bigger than a currant. You give it to Jean Baptiste, who spits it out.

The men's feet are blistered, bruised, and cut. Lewis puts medicine on the feet of his men at night.

Your own feet are bruised from walking over flint. Your own feet are sore from the thorns of the prickly pear.

You see the blisters, those small suns that burn the island of the foot.

The Indians set the plains on fire to alarm distant tribes. Then they flee behind the mountains. You know there are mountains and more mountains beyond the ones you see. You hear Lewis wonder what causes the fires.

Mosquitos troublesome, he says he writes.

The men kill two swans and sandhill cranes. Seaman, Lewis's dog, catches geese.

You pass through rough country with the men. Then the river enters an open plain. You feel the empty-earth-lodge-you-are-without-others-who-are-like-you. But it is not the Mandan village you think of. It is farther back than that. It is Shoshoni—who do not build an earth lodge, but teepee, the top pointed as the front of the canoe you paddle.

You remember the place-you-are-from. Not yet. But near it. You have been here. You know the land.

You feel the empty earth lodge swallow you. You feel hurt for all you have left.

The men are discouraged. They are afraid there are more rapids or falls. You tell them the river continues as it is. You tell the men the three forks are near.

You could sing your spirit song for them. They would hear it, but they would not know what it meant.

The men fly flags on the canoes so the Indians (if they would see them) would know they were not Indian.

[Clark]
Thursday July 25th 1805
a fine morning we proceeded on a fiew miles to the three forks of the Missouri those three forks are nearly of a Size, the North fork appears to have the most water and must be Considered as the one best calcultated for us to assend... the Indian have latterly Set the Prairies on fire, the Cause I can't account for. I saw one horse track going up the river, about four or 5 days past. after Brackfast (which we made on the ribs of a Buck killed yesterday), I wrote a note informing Capt Lewis the rout I intended to take... Shabano our Interpreter nearly tired [out] one of his ankles failing him. The bottoms are extensive and tolerable land covered with tall grass & prickly pears. The river verry much divided by Islands, Some Elk Bear & Deer and Some small timber on the Island. Great quantities of Currents, red black yellow, Purple, also Mountain Currents... Choke Cheries, Boin roche... Musquetos [and knats] verry troublesom...

They name the three forks of the Missouri, the Jefferson, the Madison, and the Gallatin after some of their leaders.

You hide your memories.
They are the herds of buffalo, coyote, wolf.
Some of the memories are grizzlies. It takes the shots of many guns to kill.

You see Toussaint struggling in the water.
What is he doing there?
You know he cannot swim.

You watch Clark struggle to pull Toussaint from the water.

What would Jean Baptiste and you do without Toussaint?

[Lewis]
Friday July 26th 1805
Set out early this morning and as usual current strong with frequent riffles... the high lands are... covered with... dry low sedge and... grass... the seeds of which are armed with a long twisted hard beard... with stiff little bristles... which penetrate our mockersons and leather legings and give us great pain untill they are removed... my poor dog suffers with them excessivley and is constantly binting and scratching himself as if in a rack of pain... found a deer's skin which had been left by Capt. C. with a note informing me of his having met with a horse but had seen no fresh appearance of the Indians... This morning Capt Clark left Sharbono and Joseph Fields at the camp of last evening and proceeded up the river about 12 miles to the top of a mountain... rejoined Sharbono and Fields... Capt C. so unwell that he felt no inclination to eat... after a short respite he resumed his march pass[ed] the North fork at a large island; here Charbono was very near being swept away by the current and cannot swim, Capt. C however risqued him [self] and saved his life.

When Clark is sick, you help construct a bower for him because the leather tent is hot in the sun.

There are showers.

The hunters return with eight deer and two elk.

You feel your own fever, but you sing it a song to go away.

The present camp is on the place where the Hidatsa took you.
You are one-who-was-taken.
You have returned.

[Lewis]
Sunday July 28th 1805.
...Our present camp is precisely on the spot that the Snake Indians were encamped at the time the Minnetares [Hidatsa] of the Knife R. first came in sight of them five years since. from hence they retreated about three miles up Jeffersons river and concealed themselves in the woods, the Minnetares pursued, attacked them killed 4 men 4 women a number of boys, Sah-cah-gar-we-ah o[u]r Indian woman was one of the female prisoners taken at that time; tho' I cannot discover that she shews any immotion of sorrow in recollecting this event, or of joy in being again restored to her native country; if she has enough to eat and a few trinkets to wear I believe she would be perfectly content anywhere.

You dream your legs are oars.
You are rowing,
running from the Hidatsa.
It's the ghost horses you see again.
They take you from the Shoshoni.
The horses are cutting you in half.
You cry in a place the men cannot see.
You see Otter Woman's hand stretched out to you.

Each day you break camp, travel a few miles, make camp again for the night.

Some of the men are lame with stone bruises.

Toussaint still complains of his legs.

[Lewis]
Tuesday July 30th 1805
Sharbono, his woman and two invalleds and myself walked through the bottom of the Lard side of the river about 4 1/2 miles when we again struck it at the place the woman informed us that she was taken prisoner. Here we halted untill Capt Clark arrived which was not untill after one P.M. the water being strong and the river extreemly crooked.

Would he have you carry him if you could?

The tumor on Clark's foot *discharges a considerable quantity of matter.*

Drewyer is disabled by a fall.

Lewis pulls the man's shoulder back into its socket again.

Even Seaman limps.

There are small rapids which are difficult to pass that you didn't remember. The river bed is broken by gravelly bars and divided by islands. There are strong currents.

You see the men drag the canoes over shoals. They are unable to walk on shore because of the brush; they have to wade in the foaming river and haul the boats by their

cords. They soon grow fatigued; often falling over the slippery stones.
One canoe nearly overturns.

You unpack the baggage that is wet and let it dry.
Some of the canisters of powder are spoiled, but others stayed dry.

You dig in the honey-suckle, rosebush, currant, serviceberry, and goose-berry bushes.

> [Clark]
> August 7th Wednesday 1805
> all Streams Contain emence number of Beaver orter Musk-rats &c

Sometimes you know Otter Woman is with you. She is from here too. You leave part of yourself wherever you go; wherever-something-happens-that-takes-something-from-you.

You see Beaverhead, the place you are from.
There is a storm inside you.
The hollow earth lodge inside you enlarges to swal-low the land and its air.

Your people are near though you don't see them yet.

> [Lewis]
> Thursday August 8th 1805
> ...the Indian woman recognized the point of a high plain to our right which she informed us was not very distant from the sum-mer retreat of her nation on a river beyond the mountains which runs to the west. the hill she says her nation calls the beaver's head from a conceived re[se]blance of it's figure to the head of that animal. she assures us that we shall either find her people on this river or on the river immediately west of it's source; which from it's present size cannot be very distant...

It is here that Lewis goes ahead. You want to go. You are near the Shoshoni. You don't want to wait. But you are left behind.

Now you travel forward with Clark.

You remember the tribe. How you were nothing to them either. The women work. They do what they are told.

> [Lewis]
> Sunday August 11th 1805
> After having marched for five miles I discovered an Indian on horse back about two miles distant coming down the plain toward us. With my glass I discovered from his dress that he was of a different nation from any that we had yet seen, and was satisfyed of his being a Sosone.

> [Lewis]
> Wednesday August 14th
> ...this evening Charbono struck his indian Woman for which Capt C. gave him a severe repremand.

You cross a small stream and there is Lewis with some of the Shoshoni.
You suck your fingers to show they are your tribe.

A girl runs toward you. She is a girl you know. She was taken by the Hidatsa also, but escaped. You are singing and she is singing with you. The others sing until the parts of your singing join.

hey hey hey
hey hey hey hey hi

You hear your own language in your ears. You spoke it quietly to Otter Woman. Now you hear it in the air. You have returned to the place you are from. The distance in you shuts.

The girl holds Jean Baptiste. You see him laugh.

You tell the girl about Otter Woman.
You ask about the others.

You follow Lewis and the Shoshoni into camp.
You see Drewyer dressed like a Shoshoni.

[Lewis]
Saturday August 17th 1805
...Shortly after Capt Clark arrived with the Interpreter Charbono, and the Indian woman, who proved to be a sister of the Chief Cameahwait. The meeting of those people was really affecting, particularly between Sah-cah-gar-we-ah and and an Indian woman, who had been taken prisoner at the same time with her and who, had afterwards escaped from the Minnetares [Hidatsa] and rejoined her nation... we unloaded our canoes and... formed a canopy of one of our large sails... for the Indians to set under while we spoke to them... about 4. P.M. we called them together and through the medium of Labuish, Charbono and Sah-cah-gar-weah, we communicated to them fully the objects which had brought us into this distant part of the country... we also gave them as a reason why we wished to pe[ne]trate the country as far as the ocean to the west of them was to examine and find out a more direct way to bring merchandize to them... [we asked for] horses to transport our baggage without which we could not subsist, and... a pilot to conduct us through the mountains was also necessary... but... we did not ask their horses or

their services without giving satisfactory compensation in return... we gave him [Cameahwait] a medal... with the likeness of Mr Jefferson the President of the U' States in releif on one side and clasp hands with the pipe and tomahawk on the other... to the other chiefs we gave each a small medal which were struck in the Presidency of George Washing[ton] Esqr.

Lewis and Clark sit you in a council. You have not spoken in council before. Women are not allowed. Lewis tells you what to say. You look at the chief as you speak. It is Cameahwait, your brother. You recognize him before he recognizes you. You jump up; throw your blanket over him. Something in you breaks; you cry. He says your name in Shoshoni, *Boat Pusher*.

You see Cameahwait's hair is short. You know the Hidatsa have raided the camp again, and killed more Shoshoni.
You ask about the others. Your parents and everyone but two brothers and the son of an oldest sister are dead. Your other brother is not here at this time.

You see the hungry faces of your people. You know what it is to eat roots and berries. You know what it is to fear.

You see them look at Seaman, but you tell them he is not for eating.

You sit down to speak again. You try to translate for Lewis and Clark, but your voice is a river through a narrow canyon with sharp rocks in it. The rocks tear your words. You swallow. You wait. You swallow again.

You continue translating.

Lewis and Clark ask Cameahwait about the country ahead. Cameahwait tells them the river passes through perpendicular cliffs. It is full of rapids and falls. There is no deer, elk, or any game. There is not sufficient timber to build canoes. You see the faces of Lewis and Clark. They do not want to hear. Cameahwait should tell them they are nearing winter. The mountains are full of snow.

[Lewis]
Saturday August 17th 1805 [continued]
...we gave the 1st Chief an uniform coat shirt a pair of scarlet legings a carrot of tobacco and some small articles to each of the other we gave a shi[r]t leging[s] handkerchief a knife some tobacco and a few small articles we also distributed a good quantity paint mockerson awles knives beads looking-glasses &c among the other Indians and gave them a plentifull meal of lyed (hull taken off by being boiled in lye) corn which ws the first they had ever eaten in their lives... every article about us appeared to excite astonishment in their minds; the appearance of the men, their arms, the canoes, our manner of working them, the b[l]ack man york and the sagacity of my dog were equally objects of admiration. I also shot my air-gun which was so perfectly incomprehensible that they immediately denominated it the great medi-

It is the smell of the trees
you remember.
The cedar, spruce, pine.
It is the smell of trees that
makes you cry.

cine. The idea which the indians
mean to convey this apellation is
something that eminates from or
acts immediately by the influence
or power of god is manifest by it's
incomprehensible power of
action... To keep the indians in
good humour you must not
fatique them with too much busi-
ness at one time. Therefore after
the council we gave them to eat
and amused them a while by
shewing them such articles as
we thought would be entertain-
ing to them, and then renewed
our enquiries with rispect to
the country.

[Lewis]
Monday August 19th 1805
... I was anxious to learn whether
these people had the venerial,
and made the enquiry through
the intrepreter and his wife; the
information was that they sometimes had it but I could not learn
their remedy; they most usually
die with it's effects. This seems a
strong proof that these disorders
bothe ganaraehah [gonorrhea]
and Louis Venerae are native
disorders of of America.

You adopt your sister's son.
You want to stay with the
Shoshoni and raise Jean
Baptiste and your nephew,
but you know Toussaint
won't let you.

Lewis and Clark open and air all their baggage. They soak
animal skins in water and cut them into cords to tie the
baggage to the horses.
Cameahwait and others have agreed to lead them for a ways.

Before you were taken by the Hidatsa, you were already promised to a man, who would have been a husband. He is old now. He has other wives. He sees your baby. He sees you are taken by Toussaint Charbonneau. He releases you.

You want to stay with the Shoshoni. You have always wanted to return. But you do not have a Shoshoni husband. Your brother is chief. You could stay with him. Or your other brother when he returns. But you have a husband. You are traveling with the explorers.

At night you see the teepees lit with the fire inside them. The light through the hides makes them look like moons, only folded to a point on top.

At night when Toussaint sleeps, you cry as you feed Jean Baptiste. You remember how the Hidatsa ripped you from the stream. You see how the Maker might have allowed you to be taken. Something larger was coming. The white men who would take your land. They are here now. You choose to go with them. You choose to follow.

This earth that pulls you apart.
This place under the moon.

Lewis puts you on a horse. The Shoshoni look. The women always walk. The women will not like you. You leave your sister's son. You leave your village. This time by choice.

Cameahwait and two other Shoshoni chiefs go with you as guides. A few other Shoshoni come also. And some women.

The explorers meet Indians as they travel. Lewis spends a great deal of time writing about them in his journal. Their moccasins sewn with porcupine quills, their shells

> [Lewis]
> Wednesday August 21st 1805
> This morning was very cold. the ice 1/4 of an inch thick on the water which stood in the vessels exposed to the air. some wet deerksins that had been spread on the grass last evening are stiffly frozen. the ink f[r]eizes in my pen...

of the *perl oister* they get from tribes who live near the Ocean, the elk teeth sewn on the women's dresses, their fox and otter tails, their bird claws and bear claws, their plaited grasses, their feathers and beads. Lewis spends all day writing. He draws the baskets the Indians use as fish traps.

You want to tell him he should get across the mountains.

You are ready to leave and Drewyer finds an Indian stole his gun. You wait as he rides after him and returns sometime later with his gun.

> [Lewis]
> August 23rd Friday 1805
> ...I proceeded on. Sometimes in a Small wolf parth & other times Climbing over rocks for 12 miles...

Now you travel with the men and women. You come upon another tribe who are afraid of the explorers. The women and children cry. They are inconsolable because they have never seen white men. Then they see the Shoshoni men and women and you pass with them. They see Jean Baptiste.

Now the path is steep. The horses fall backward down the cliffs. The river below foams and beats the rocks in its path. It is nearly impossible to descend the river or *clamber* over the mountain. You remember the ghost horses. You wish you had wings.

You tell Toussaint that Cameahwait is leaving with a party of Indians who will show up. He does nothing with the information.

Now Lewis is angry. He calls the Chiefs together and smokes the pipe with them.

He reasons with them. Why had they requested their people meet them? Lewis would not have attempted to cross the mountains if they had not promised to give their assistance. If they don't help, he will turn around

[Lewis]
Sunday August 25th 1805
...sometime after we had halted, Charbono mentioned to me with apparent unconcern that he expected to meet all the Indians from the camp on the Columbia tomorrow on their way to the Missouri. allarmed at this information I asked why he expected to meet them. he then informed me that the 1st Chief had dispatched some of his young men... requesting the Indians to meet them tomorrow... and consequently leave me and my baggage on the mountain... I was out of patience with the folly of Charbono who had not sufficient sagacity to see the consequencies which would inevitably flow from such a movement of the indians, and altho' he had be in possession of this information since early in the morning when it had been communicated to him by his Indian woman yet he never mentioned it untill the after noon...

and they will never see anymore white men in their country. If they wish the white men to be their friends and to assist them against their enemies by giving them arms, then they should not promise anything they could not do. Lewis tells them they have seen how he shares the meat his hunters kill. He will continue to share the meat they have. If they intend to keep their promise, they should dispatch one of their young men immediately with an order to their people to remain where they were. The two inferior chiefs say they wish to be good as their word. Cameahwait is silent for some time, then says he knew he has done wrong, but is concerned that his people are hungry. He says he wants to keep his word. Lewis calls the women and men who have been assisting him in the transportation of his baggage and they agree to continue for a ways.

You are with the women when you stop. One of them is going to have a baby and you wait with her. You hold her hand, remembering your own pain. You feel panic, but you do not tell her. You think of the ghost horses; you feel like you fall over a cliff into the river. But she has the baby quickly, slick and wet as an otter, and catches up with the men.

You show Jean Baptiste the baby. He doesn't know what to do. He puts his fingers in his mouth and hides his head on your shoulder.

Lewis and Clark make their plans. You like to hear them talk. They say what they want to happen. With their words, they say the different ways to make it happen. They are not driven here and there without thinking. You watch them *calculate*.

There is nothing to eat but chokecherry and red haw. When one of his men is sick, Lewis gives him his horse to ride. When one deer is killed, Lewis gives his meat to the Indian women who carry some of his baggage. The women look at you. These are the men you travel with.

Lewis asks Cameahwait for twenty more horses for packing and for eating, if necessary. Cameahwait tells him the Hidatsa took many of their horses in the last raid. They talk more until Cameahwait sells him the horses.

Now Lewis and Clark have their plans in order. That evening, Lewis directs the fiddle to be played and the white men dance. The Indians look at them amazed. They do not dance like any animal or bird; they do not dance for a reason. They dance to dance. The Indians look with amusement.

In the morning, the Indians return to the Shoshoni camp, except Toby, an old guide, and his son. You hide your head on the shoulders of the women. You cover your brother with your blanket. You do not look back when they leave.

In one afternoon: Snow. Rain. Sleet.
The buffalo road follows the ridges instead of the valleys. Toby, the Shoshoni guide, gets lost. The explorers backtrack three miles. The road is steep, stony. The men are hungry. They camp at an old Indian fishing camp. They name the creek *Colt-Killed-Creek*.

As you continue, the guide tells Lewis and Clark the Missouri is just over a mountain road. They have taken four weeks instead of four days because they made the long loop south to the Shoshoni camp.

[Clark]
Wednesday (Sunday) Sept 15th 1805
...Several horses Sliped and roled down Steep hills which hurt them verry much the one which Carried my desk & Small trunk Turned over & roled down a mountain 40 yards & lodged against a tree, broke the Desk the horse escaped and appeared but little hurt Some others verry much hurt, from this point I observed a range of high mountains Covered with Snow from SE. To SW with their tops bald... of timber...

You are into winter in the moutains. The country is rugged. Timber has fallen across the path. The men chop their way through the brush and undergrowth.

Snow is above your ankles. Sometimes the path is hard to find.
You think of nothing but climbing.

At night, you feel your ache.

The men eat dried fish and camas roots. They are sick. They buy dogs from the Indians to eat. Sometimes they kill a horse. Sometimes they shoot a pheasant.

There are mountains and mountains on all sides.

The men wrap rags around their feet.

You wrap another hide around Jean Baptiste.

There is nothing to eat.

> [Clark]
> October 6th Saturday [Sunday] 1805
> ...I am taken verry unwell with a pain in the bowels & Stomach, which is certainly the effets of my diet...

Lewis and Clark see how many mountains there are.

You climb the Bitterroots with Jean Baptiste.

At night you eat their portable soup, mixed with snow and heated.

The men look half-starved. They are weak.

Lewis makes a new map. He covers the Northwest Passage with crooked lines of mountains.

He looks at you a moment, but you cannot tell him how many there are.

Now you come to the tribe of the Nez Perce.

You see the Indians take Lewis's tomahawk. With sign language you tell them not to steal.

> [Clark]
> October 8th Tuesday 1805
> ...had everything opened, and two Sentinels put over them to keep off the Indians who are enclined to theave haveing Stole Serveral Small articles those people appeared disposed to give us every assistance in their power during our distress.

You know Jean Baptiste is cranky because your milk is thin.

You know the men are vulnerable because they are half-starved. The Nez Perce could kill them. But an old woman, Watkuweis, tells them a story of how she had been saved by a white man when she was a young woman. Twisted Hair, the Nez Perce chief, listens to her voice.

The Nez Perce give the men camas root and dried fish. The men gorge themselves because they are hungry. Now they are sick. Even Seaman, the dog, is sick. You hear him vomit. Then he returns to watch over the men. Lewis pets him when he licks his face.

When the men are better, the Nez Perce teach Lewis and Clark how to make canoes by burning out the logs instead of chopping, which saves their energy.

An Indian Woman acts crazy. Lewis and Clark write her in their words. But they do not think why. They do not think she may be testing these new men to see what they will do. To see who they are.

A fear comes over you. You fight it away. The enormous mountains could eat you with their teeth. They are ghost horses also. You pass through the wavy parts. The evil spirits try to make you dance. You think maybe

[Clark]
October 9th Wednesday 1805
...at Dark we were informed that our old guide & his son had left us and had been Seen running up the river Several miles above, we could not account for the cause of his leaveing us at this time, without receiving his pay for the services he had rendered us... Or letting us know of his intentions. we requested a Chief to Send a horseman after our old guide to come back and receive his pay &c. which he advised us not to as his nation would take his things from him before he passed their camps... a woman faind madness &c. &c...

it was the spirits that made the woman mad. You think of the unknown travel. The risk. Yet Lewis and Clark and the men, who are sick and weak, push on.

Lewis and Clark ask the Nez Perce to keep their horses until they return in the spring. The men mark the horses so they can remember which are theirs.

The red rocks stand up as if they are trees.
You watch the swirl of water around the rocks.
The lap of waves on the shore.

Once again, the travel is by water.
As you row you remember your name, *Boat Pusher*.
As you row, you push the boat with your oar. You know the Maker knew you would be taken from the Shoshoni. You know the Maker named you *this*.

They call the rivers Clearwater,
Snake.
In the distance
the Salmon.

[Clark]
October 13th Sunday 1805
The wife of Shabono our interpreter we find reconsiles all the Indians, as to our friendly intentions a woman with a party of men is a token of peace...

[Clark]
October 14th Monday 1805
a verry Cold morning wind from the West and Cool untill about 12 oClock when it Shifted to the S.W. at 2 1/2 miles passed a remarkable rock verry large and resembling the hill [hull] of a Ship Situated on a Lard point at some distance... passed rapids at 6 and 9 miles. at 12 miles we came too at the head of a rapid which the Indians told me was verry bad, we viewed the rapid found it bad in decending three Stern Canoes stuck fast for some time... here we dined, and for the first time for three weeks past I had a good dinner of Blue wing Teal, after dinner we Set out and had not proceded on two miles before our Stern Canoe in passing thro a Short rapid opposit the head of an Island, run on a Smothe rock and turned board Side... The canoe filed and sunk a number of articles floated out, Such as the mens bedding clothes & skin.

On the shore is a parcel of split timber left while the Indians *are out hunting Antelope in the plains*. Here you see Lewis and Clark take the Indians' wood. For the first time they take the property of the Indians without their consent. The night is cold and the men *make use of part of the boards and split logs for fire wood*.

Jean Baptiste stirs in the night.
You nurse him and he sleeps.

In the day, his head darts from the new bier you make him like a *petite chienne*.

Now a canoe runs onto a rock when you are almost through the rapids. Three other canoes stop and the men unload the grounded canoe. They pull it off the rock and then proceed.

Seaman sits in the front of a dugout, nose to the wind, as though a guide for the explorers.

You see the eyes of Indians inflamed from looking into the sun on water while they fish. Many of them do not see you.

What is it you did not see? You would have to leave the Shoshoni village again? Your ache would not go away?

[Clark]
October 17th Thursday 1805
Capt Lewis took a Vocabulary of the Languages of those people who call themselves Sakulk... Those people as also those of the flat heads which we had passed on the Koskoske and the Lewis's rivers are subject to sore eyes, and many are blind of one and Some of both eyes. this misfortune must be owing to the reflections of the sun &c. on the waters in which they are continually fishing during the Spring Summer & fall, & the snows dureing the, winter Seasons, in this open countrey where the eye has no rest...

Lewis and Clark meet with the Flatheads, give them metals to trade for horses. This is how it goes: Their conversation with the Tushepaws is held through a boy whom they find among them— Clark speaks in English to Labieche—who translates it to Toussaint in French—who tells it to you in Minnetaree [Hidatsa]—you in Shoshoni to the boy—the boy in Tushepaw to that nation.

That is how it is done.

The Indians surround the explorers. They come in canoes. They stand on the cliffs. Lewis has a council with some of them. He tells them of his friendly intentions toward them and all the *red children*. At one place, four men in a canoe come from a large encampment on an Island on the River, stop, look at the men for a moment, and turn around without speaking a word to them.

Lewis and Clark buy dogs and wood and fish (when the fish are not rotten).
Does Seaman know the men kill the dogs?
Does he turn his back to the knowing?
He does not fear being eaten. He knows he will not be among the dogs who are killed.

Now the Columbia.

The men do not show relief to be on this last river that will take them to the ocean. Maybe they are relieved and don't show it. They only push on with determination.

Even Jean Baptiste is restless. He doesn't like his small sack, or the small space in the boat, but wants to climb over whatever he can.

Clark shoots some birds which fall from the sky. The Indians think the explorers fall out of the clouds. They are afraid of the noise of the guns. They are afraid of the white men.

They stay in their lodges and cry and wring their hands. Lewis calms them with tokens and his quiet words.

The tribes watch you pass from the shore. The women look at you. The men. What kind of party is this that takes a woman and baby with them? Not a war party. Not anyone who came to harm.

[Clark]
October 18th Friday 1805
...we thought it necessary to lay in a Store of Provisions for our voyage, and the fish being out of Season, we purchased forty dogs for which we gave articles of little value, such as bells, thimbles, knitting pins, brass wire and a few beeds... everything arranged we took in our Two Chiefs, and set out on the great Columbia river, haveing left our guide and the two young men two of them enclined not to proceed on any further, and the 3d could be of no service to us as he did not know the river below...

[Clark]
October 19th Saturday 1805
...the Indians came out & Set by me and smoked. They said we came from the clouds &c. &c. and were not men &c &c... As Soon as they Saw the Squar wife of the interperter they pointed to her... they imediately all came out and appeared to assume new life, the sight of This Indian woman, wife to one of our interprts confirmed those people of our friendly intentions, as no woman ever accompanies a war party of Indians in this quarter...

The woman and baby do not go into battle. So this party is safe. The explorers put you at the head of the party. When they don't need you, you walk behind. They should hear your song. It is on your wings they ride. A small bird for such a large hunting party.

The old chiefs who act as guide want to leave. There is rumor of Indian wars and they don't want to be killed. The men are uneasy.

You look down into the river between two rocks. You see the boils and swells and whirlpools. The same as in the tribes.

The rapids are impossible to portage. You bind Jean Baptiste to your chest and you ride.

[Clark]
October 23rd Wednesday 1805
...Great numbers of Sea Otters in the river below the falls, I shot one in the narrow chanel to day which I could not get. Great numbers of Indians visit us both from above and below. one of the old Chiefs who had accompanied us from the head of the river, informed us that he herd the Indians Say that the nation below intended to kill us. we examined all the arms &c. complete the amunition to 100 rounds. The nativs leave us earlyer this evening than usial, which gives a Shadow of conformation to the information of our old Chief, as we are at all time & places on our guard... I observed on the beach near the Indian Lodges two buti-full canoes of different Shape & Size to what we had Seen above wide in the midd[l]e and tapering to each end, on the bow curious figures were cut in the wood &c. Capt Lewis went up to the Lodges to See those Canoes and exchanged our Smallest canoe for one of them by giveing a Hatchet & a few trinkets to the owner who informed that he purchased it of a white man below for a horse, these canoes are neeter made than any I have ever Seen and calculated to ride the waves, and carry emense burthens... our two old chiefs appeared verry uneasy this evening.

You see a small wolf caught in a snare set in the willows.
It is steep, rugged, rocky country.

In the evening two chiefs and some Indians arrive with dressed elk skin, deer meat and some bread made of roots. Lewis and Clark give them medals, handkerchiefs, arm bands, and a few other trinkets.

You help the men unpack the wet baggage.

At night, Cruzatte plays his violin and the men dance *which pleases the savage.*
They like to see York dance also.

As you travel, you see houses made of cedar bark.
Lewis and Clark camp on a high rock in case the Indians attack.

Lewis makes *selestial observation*. He even writes the stars.

[Clark]
October 27th Sunday 1805
...we took a vocabelary of the Languages of the 2 nations, the one liveing at the Falls call themselves E-nee-shur. The other resideing at the levels or narrows in a village on the Std side call themselves E-chee-lute   not withstanding those people live only 6 miles apart, [they understand] but fiew words of each others language the language of those above having great similarity with those tribes of flat heads we have passed. all have the cluck-ing tone anexed which is prodominate above, all flatten the heads of their female chil-dren near the falls, and maney have follow the same custom. The language of the Che-luc-it-te-quar a fiew miles before is different from both in a small degree. The wind increased in the evening and blew verry hard from the same point W day fair and cold... Some words with Shabono about his duty...

The Indians have muskets, swords, and several *Brass Tea Kittles*.
Lewis purchases five small dogs, some dried berries and roots.

Seaman watches Jean Baptiste crawl. He wants to play with him, but you push the dog away. Seaman doesn't know how big he is, stepping on your feet with his large paws, drooling on your hand.

There is much traffic on the river. The Indians have canoes that walk on the high waves. The canoes are made of white cedar with animals carved on the bows.
The Indians wear skins of wolves, deer, elk, wild cat [lynx], fox, mountain sheep, white hare and otter. One of them wears a white man's jacket.

You feel you belong to the explorers more than you do to them.

There are many sandbars in the river.
There are many falls.

You see the drawings of men and animals. You realize it is a burying place. You take Jean Baptiste away from it.
Seaman follows.
It is too easy to step into the next world.
You don't want to get near.

[Clark]
October 31st Thursday 1805
A cloudy rainey disagreeable morning I proceeded down the river to view [the rapids] we had to pass... the Great Shute [the Cascades of the Columbia River] which commenced at the Island on which we encamped continued with great rapidity and force thro a narrow chanel much compressed... at 1/2 a mile below the end of the portage passed a house where there had been an old town for ages past as this house was old Decayed and a place of fleas I did not enter it... about 1/2 a mile below this house... is 8 Vaults... In several of these vaults the dead bodies w[e]re raped... in Skins tied... with grass and bark... laid... east & west... other Vaults containing bones only... on the tops and on poles... hung Brass kittles & frying pans pearced through the bottoms, baskets, bowls of wood, sea Shels, skins, bits of Cloth, hair, bags of Trinkets & Small pieces of bone &c... and... curious engraveing and Paintings on the boards which formed the

Vaults I observed Several wooden Images, cut in the fugure[s] of men... I also observed the remains of Vaults rotted entirely into the ground and covered with moss... This must be the burrying place for maney ages for the inhabitants of those rapids....

Lewis asks you to talk to a woman of your tribe, but you cannot understand. You were taken from the Shoshoni long ago. Words change when they are separated from one another.

You don't think she is Shoshoni anyway.

That night you cannot sleep because of the noise of swans, geese, brants, ducks, cranes, in the sandhills. At least they can talk to one another.

[Clark]
November 3rd Sunday 1805
The fog so thick this morning we did not think it prudent to set out untill 10 oClock we set out and proceeded on verry well accompanied by our Indian friends. This morning Labich killed 3 Geese flying Collins killed a Buck. This water rose___Inches last night the effects of tide... a canoe arrived with a man his wife and 3 children, and a woman whome had been taken prisoner from the Snake Inds on Clarks River. I sent the Interpreters wife who is a So so ne or Snake Indian of the Missouri, to Speake to this squar, they could not understand each other Sufficiently to converse... Indians continue to be with us, several canoes continue with us, The Indians at the last village have more cloth and Uropean trinkets than above.

You pass more Indians. You look at their canoes ornamented with bears and figures of men.

You see a mountain in the distance by itself. Lewis says it is *Mt. Helien* which may be the highest mountain in America.

Lewis and Clark try to camp away from the natives who are constantly with them, usually to steal their goods. Before the Great Falls they wanted to see the Indians. Well, now they are here.
You hear the guns of the hunters. The explorers always are in need of meat. You gather raspberries.

There is much fleas and rain.

You are not from the ocean.
You do not like the smell.
You do not know water that has no land.

> [Clark]
> November 7th Thursday 1805
> Great joy in camp we are in view of the Ocian, (in the morning when the fog clears off just below last village...) this great Pacific Octean which we had been so long anxious to See. and the roreing or noise made by the waves brakeing on the rockey Shores... may be heard distin[n]ctly... We made 34 miles to day...

The swells in the river are so high, the canoes toss back and forth. Several are very sick. You are one of them.

The water you drink tastes salty. You are sick again.

It rains.
It rains.
It rains.

You are in a country you don't know.

If there is cold weather before the men can kill and dress skins for clothing they will suffer. Some of the men cough from the cold. They lay in wet clothes all night.

[Clark]
November 12th Tuesday 1805
A Tremendious wind from the S.W. about 3 o Clock this morning with Lightineng and hard claps of Thunder, and Hail which Continued untill 6 oClock a.m. when it became light for a Short time, then the heavens became sudenly darkened by a black cloud from the S.W. and rained with great violence untill 12 oClock, the waves tremendious brakeing with great fury against the rocks and trees on which we were encamped. our Situation is dangerous... we took the advantage of low tide and moved our camp around a point to a Small wet bottom... It would be distressing to see our situation, all wet and colde our bedding also wet (and the robes of the party which compase half the bedding is rotten)...

Jean Baptiste feels warm and you worry. You think something is bothering him, but it goes away.
You see the waves. They are where the ghost horses stand up on their hind legs.

Seaman's fur is stiff from the salt water. He has fleas. He stinks.

He wants to sit beside you.

You try to comb his fur. You think the dried salt water itches. He rolls on his back. He rubs himself on the ground. He bites his fur. Jean Baptiste wants to hug him, but you hold Jean Baptiste back. Jean Baptiste fusses. He has been fussy. You want him to be quiet.

[Clark]
November 15th Friday 1805
Rained all the last night at intervales of sometimes 2 hours... eleven days of rain... I can neither hunt... or proceed on... We loaded and set out passed the blustering Point below which is a sand beech, with a small marshey bottom for 3 miles on the Stard Side, on which is a large village of 36 houses deserted by the Inds & in full possession of the flees... The tide meeting of me and the emence swells from the Main Ocian (immediately in front of us) raised to such a hite that I concluded to form a camp on the highest spot... 4 Indians in a canoe came down the papto [wapatoo] roots to sell, which they asked blankets or ropes, both of which we could not spare I informed those Indians all of which understood some English that if they stole our guns &c the men would certainly shute them, they all promised not to take any thing...

You hear Lewis call the place Cape Disappointment. He expects a ship from President Thomas Jefferson filled with clothes, trade goods, and supplies the explorers need, and no ship is here.

[Clark]
November 17th Sunday 1805
...At half past 10 Clock Capt Lewis returned haveing travesed Haley Bay to Cape Disappointment and Sea coast to the North for Some distance. Several Chinnook Indians followed Capt L, and a Canoe came up with roots mats &c. to Sell...

Clark takes some of his men to see the ocean: Sergeants Pryor, Ordway, J. Fields, R. Fields, Shannon, Colter, Bratten, Wiser, Toussaint, and York. You stay at camp with Jean Baptiste.

You are wearing your blue trade-bead belt. The Indians see your beads. You know the Indians want them. But the beads are yours. It is what Lewis and Clark would say.
You see Lewis looking at your waist. The Indians

[Clark]
Novr 20th Wednesday 1805
...maney Indians about one of which had on a robe made of 2 sea otter skins. Capt Lewis offered him many things for his skins with others a blanket a coat all of which he refused we at length purchase it for a belt of Blue Beeds which the Squar had...

want the beads because they are *ti-a-co-mo-shack*, chief beads. They are sky-beads.
You give them up.
For now, you have your place on earth.

Lewis and Clark decide to make winter camp. They know where to build it, but they let everyone vote which side of the bay. They call each of our names. Even York. Even Sacajawea.

Why can't they go inland for winter? You ask Toussaint. They still think a ship might come, he tells you.

Lewis names the winter camp Fort Clatsop. He claims the Clatsop name for his.

Rain.
Rain.
Rain.

[Clark]
November 21st Thursday 1805
...Several Indians and squars came this evening   I beleave for the purpose of gratifying the passion of our men, Those people appear to view sensuality as a necessary evill... The young women sport openly with our men... maney of the women are handsom... The women ware a string of something curious tied tight above the ankle, all have large swelled legs & thighs They live on Elk, Deer, fowls, but priniciplaly fish and roots of 3 kinds. Lickorish, Wapto &c... Pocks & venereal is common amongst them... I saw one man & one woman who appeared to be all in scabs & several men with the venereal their other Disorder and the remides for them I could not learn...

You watch Lewis draw his plan for Fort Clatsop. He draws two rows of three rooms each, and joins them with a wall. This fort has four sides, while Fort Mandan had three.

The men cut logs for the winter camp at Fort Clatsop. Other men split the logs. You hear the *clop* of their axes through the woods.

The fleas are troublesome.

You listen to the *clunk* of
their axes.

[Clark]
Saturday 30th November 1805
...Some men Complain of a
looseness and griping which I
contribute to the diet, pounded
fish mixed with Salt water, I
directed that in future that the
party mix the pounded fish with
fresh water. The squar gave me a
piece of bread made of flour
which She had reserved for her
child and carefully Kept untill
this time, which had unfortunate-
ly got wet, and a little Sour. this
bread I ate with great satisfaction,
it being the only mouthfull I had
tasted for Several months past.
my hunters killed three Hawks...
They Saw 3 Elk but could not get
a Shot at them. They fowlers
killed 3 black Ducks with Sharp
white beeks...

You walk with Jean Bap-
tiste on the wet mat of leaves.

At the spring you get water.

More rain and rain.

[Clark]
Tuesday 24th December 1805
Some hard rain at Different times
last night, and moderately this
morning without intermition all
hands employed in carrying
Punchens & finishing covering
the huts, and the greater part of
the men move into them a hard
rain in the evening...

The trees are close together. Their trunks are like the legs of tall
animals. You remember the story of the *lone man* who built an
ark for the Mandan during the flood. You think of him as the

long man who walked above the flood. Maybe these *long animals* are his.

Maybe they walked through the flood with the ark that held the Mandan.

Maybe the ocean is part of that flood.

Jean Baptiste sees a chipmunk and tries to squirm out of his pack.
You let him play in the fern and huckleberry.
None of the chipmunks come out of hiding.
You listen to the birds fuss.
Somewhere, you hear Seaman bark.

You know it is a medicine day for the explorers. You have nothing but weasel tails to give.

Your fingers are cold. Jean Baptiste's nose is running.

It is damp. Chilly.

Smoke from the fires fills the hut. Your eyes burn. You hear the men cough. You cough.

The fleas bite.

[Clark]
Christmas Wednesday 25th December 1805
at day light this morning we we[re] awoke by the discharge of the fire arm[s] of all our party & a Selute, Shouts and a Song which the whole party joined in under our windows... I recved a pres[e]nt of Capt L. of a fleece hosrie [hosiery] Shirt Draws and Socks, a pr Mockerson of White-house a Small Indian basket of Gutherich, two Dozen white weazils tails of the Indian woman... we would have spent this day the nativity of Christ in feasting, had we any thing either to raise our Sperits or even gratify our appetites, our Diner concist-ed of pore Elk, so much Spoiled that we eate it thro' necessity, Some Spoiled pounded fish and a fiew roots.

You hear Lewis talk to his men. They must keep on guard against the Indians and never forget their guard.

He says the Indians seem friendly and likeable, but they are greedy and steal. They will take what is not theirs without asking.

Captain Lewis is despondent.
When Lewis's dark thoughts are where he can see them, he can cross. But it is those thoughts inside him, those horses falling into the rocks that bother Lewis.

In a dream, you see his ghost horse.

You know the weight of what he carries.

You hear him tell his men what there is to be done.

This *Captain Merry*.

[Clark]
Monday 30th December 1805
we had a Sumptious Supper of Elks tongues & marrow bones which was truly gratifying. our fortification is completed this evening and at Sun set we let the nativs know that our Custom will be in future, to Shut the gates at Sun Set at which time all Indians must go out of the fort and not return into it untill next morning...

[Lewis]
Fort Clatsop 1806 Wednesday the 1st of January
This morning I was awoke by the discharge of a Volley of Small arms, which were fired by our party in front of our quarters to usher in the new year, this was the only mark of respect which we had in our power to pay this Selibrated day. our repast of this day tho' better than that of Christmas consisted principally in the anticipation of the 1st day of January 1807, when in the bosom of our friends we hope to participate in the mirth and hilarity of the day...

The Clatsop Indians bring some roots and berries. They bring three dogs and a small piece of blubber they got from the *Killamuck*. Blubber? Lewis asks. They tell him there is a whale on the beach.

In the evening, Clark decides to take two canoes and twelve men to find the whale.

You do not like the ocean, but you want to go see the large fish. The men prepare to go. Clark calls his men. He looks past you without seeing. He knows you want to go. But he does not consider you. You are nothing he wants.

You walk from the fort. You leave Jean Baptiste sleeping.
Your eyes fill with anger.
You have walked as one of them. You have told the Indians the explorers were not a war party. They just want to pass through the land. Do Lewis and Clark know what the Indians could do to them? Do they know how feeble and few the explorers are?

You hit the tree. You bang it with your weight.
Your legs fall to the ground.
You found roots and berries for them. You showed them what they did not see.
You spoke to the Shoshoni for them.
You left the Shoshoni for them.

They do not know the weight you carry.

You become a ghost horse. You feel the waves rise.
You could pound them like a storm.

What should you do? You know the way Lewis holds his anger. His feelings. You know Clark does not have them like Lewis does. You will give Clark yours.
You return to the fort. Your voice is shaking. You speak to Clark.
You *insist* you go with them.

These men who name the water.

The ocean is where the water goes on and on.

You see the place where the ghost horses stand up.

At the ocean, the ghost horses are white.

You push Jean Baptiste into his sack so the wind won't get his ears.

[Lewis]
Monday January 6th 1806
Capt Clark set out after an early breakfast with the party in two canoes... Charbonoe and his Indian woman were also of the party; the Indian woman was very impo[r]tunate to be permitted to go, and was therefore indulged; she observed that she had traveled a long way with us to see the great waters, and that now that monstrous fish was also to be seen, she thought it very hard she could not be permitted to see either (she had never yet been to the Ocean)...

The immense waves break on the shore. Pounding with anger that they have to stop. They cannot go on and run over the land. The Maker lifts the land and they cannot cross.

The ocean is like an animal skin being shaken out.

You know the Indians must have old stories of the war between the water and the land. You want to ask, but the Clatsop, Chinooks, Killamax, are boiling blubber, Clark says.

> [Clark]
> Wednesday 8th January 1806
> ...[I] thank providence for directing the whale to us; and think him more kind to us than he was to jonah, having sent this Monster to be Swallowed by us in Sted of Swallowing of us as jonah's did...

You show the whale to Jean Baptiste.

The rib bones arc on the shore. The Indians take everything else.

The bones are like the teepee poles of the Shoshoni, you tell Jean Baptiste.

The poles hold up the hide.

On the way back, one of the women, coming down a steep part of the mountain, slips and the load slides off her back. She holds to strap on the load with one hand, clings to a bush by the other. Clark rushes to help her because he is at the front of the party. He tries to hold the load until the woman could get a foot hold, but finds the load so heavy he can't hold it. It takes Clark and the husband of the woman to lower the load and give it again to the woman.

There, he sees what she carries. Maybe he will know.

At Fort Clatsop, Lewis and Clark see the torn sleeves on their men. They see the threads hanging loose from trousers. They set the men to work making new clothes from hides.

Lewis does not tan and sew. He is planning his trip back. He is going through this waiting called *patience*.

You remember winter at the Mandan village. How you watched the boys slide down the river embankment on sleds made of buffalo ribs. You remember their laugh. You think of the ribs of the whale you can tell them about.
You remember the cold of winter camp, the warm earth lodges of the Mandan.
The cache of dried beans, corn, sunflower, and squash. The roots and berries.
The firewood stacked by the wall, the mortar and pestles for grinding corn.

Even the best horses are kept in the earth lodges.

You remember the mounds of lodges look like buffalo humps as you came up the embankment from the frozen river.

Even the earth lodges have spirits.

You are hungry for corn. You dream of corn, but you see the kernels are blisters. You see the ears of corn are feet.

You watch Lewis make his *lists*:

Of Domestic Animals Horses, Dogs, and Mules with Spanish brands
Of Wild Animals Black Bear, the Elk, the Common red Deer, the
Mule deer, the black tailed Deer, the large brown Wolf, the Small
Wolf of the Plains, the large Wolf of the Plains, the tiger cat, the com-
mon red fox, the black fox, the Silver fox, large red fox of the plains,
small fox of the plains, or Kit fox, Antilope, Sheep, beaver, common
otter, sea otter, minks, seals, racoons, large Grey Squirrel, Sewelel,
Braro, rat, mouse, mole, hare, rabbet, and pole Cat or skunk.
Of Indians Chopunnish, Sokulks, Cutssahnims, Chymnapum,
E[c]helutes, Eneshuh & Chilluckkittequaws
Then he says something about them.
That is how he writes with his head in his pages all day.

You think sometimes he is feverish.

There is a damp chill that does not leave.

You still think the trunks of the trees are the legs of large
animals. You look up to see their heads as you carry water
from the nearby springs.

The leaves on the path *splot* with drops of rain off the trees.

You hear the creak of the gate to the fort closing at night.

> [Lewis]
> Friday February 14th 1806
> ...Capt Clark completed a map of
> the country through which we
> have been passing from Fort
> Mandan to this place. in this map
> the Missouri Jefferson's river the
> S.E. branch of the Columbia,

As Lewis reviews the way they had taken, he concludes Jefferson's instructions to follow the Missouri to its headwaters had been the longest route, and they should have traveled overland from the Great Falls to the Bitterroot valley, avoiding Three Forks, Lemhi Pass, and the Salmon River. He decides on the return, when they reach Traveler's Rest, they would cross the mountains, taking different ways.

Kooskooske and columbia from the entrance of the S.E. fork to the pacific Ocean as well as part of Flathead (Clarks) river and our tract across the Rocky Mountains are laid down by celestial observation and survey. we now discover that we have found the most practicable and navigable passage across the Continent... it is that which we traveled with the exception of... the entrance of Dearborn's River untill we arrived at the Flat-head (Clarks) river at the entrance of Travelers rest creek; the distance between those two points would be traveled more advantageously by land as the navigation of the Missouri above the river Dearborn is laborious and 420 miles distant by which no advantage is gained... the most practiable rout across the continent is by way of the Missouri (falls of Missouri) to the entrance of Dearborn's river... from there to flathead (Clarks) river (by land to) the entrance of Traveller's rest Creek, from thence up Traveller's rest creek to the forks, [across] a range of mounttains which divides the waters of the two forks of this creek, and which still continuing it's Westwardly course divides the waters of the two forks of the Kooskooske river to their junction; from thence to decend to the S.E. branch of the Columbia, thence down... the Columbia to the Pacific Ocean.

You look for roots on the ground.
You smell deer.

Cocomol, chief of the Chinook, visits Fort Clatsop.

Your fingers always are cold. Jean Baptiste's nose is always running.

You hear the *sluck* of your moccasins on the leaves as you walk to the inlet. You feel the *clampy* air.

The reeds and grasses by the water push against one another.

You travel to salt camp by the ocean.
Joseph Fields, William Bratten, George Gibson make a stone oven. They boil water in metal *kittles* to make salt for curing meat.

What is wrong with the water that thrashes? What is it running from? You think there is something out there. You are afraid of the *smelly lake*. You want to return to Fort Clatsop. You don't like the roar of water. The laughing birds.

The fog. The fog. The fog.

You think you are something the explorers need.

You sing to Jean Baptiste.
You know the men listen.
The song is for them also.
You remember they called
you a *token of peace*.

[Lewis]
Sunday February 16th 1806
Sent Shannon Labeish and frazier on a hunting expedition up
the Kil-haw-a-nak-kle river
which discharges itself into the
head of Meriwethers Bay... Bratten is verry weak and complains
of a pain in the lower part of the
back when he moves... I gave him
barks and saltpeter. Gibsons
fever still continues obstinate
tho' not very high; we gave him a
dose of Dr. Rushes pills which in
maney instancis I have found
extreamly effecasious in fevers
which are in any measure caused
by the presence of boil.

At Fort Clatsop, you remember the buffalo-foot bones the
boys made horses for playing war and hunting. You wish
you had saved some of the small bones for Jean Baptiste.

You hear Toussaint talking of the skins these Indians wear:
sea otter, beaver, elk, deer, fox, and cat. Some have old
sailors clothes and Hudson Bay blankets. You hear
Toussaint talk of the nations that want the Oregon territory: the Russians, the Spanish, and Canadians. You hear
him talk of the race of the British and Americans for the
Columbia River.

There is no snow, but the wind feels cold as if there were snow.

You remember the Mandan village when the hunters brought meat on sleighs.
You remember the Indians watching the explorers cut their pirogues loose from the ice.

You remember making a water carrier from the heart skin of a buffalo. You remember the clear, transparent heart skin.

You want the snow.

At Fort Clatsop, even Seaman is bored. There is nothing to do.
They even brought candle molds.

They planned. They have what they need, though they've been gone longer than they knew.

They have lost no men.
(One, they said, before they got to the Mandan village. Natural causes no one could have cured.)

They passed out silk handkerchiefs for Christmas. They always have a supply of paper and ink even without the arrival of a ship.

How long did they plan for this journey before they left?

The Northwest Passage is longer, harder, more rugged than they thought.

There is no Northwest Passage. The rivers are interrupted by mountains and mountains.

The land is vast. It is a place-where-the-Maker-rests.

All this—and Bonaparte sells.

Lewis and Clark tell their men to stay away from the Indian women. Lewis healed them once with mercury salve. Do they want that again?
They treat ax wounds and dislocated shoulder.
They treat tumors, boils, strains, infected feet, rheumatism, and more venereal disease.
They wound. They heal.

The Indians follow Lewis for his good medicine.
His new magic.

Lewis and Clark say the men are healthier when they travel.

You see Lewis and Clark want to return.

Sometimes you feel your fever. Sometimes you have chills. But you do not tell them.

At salt camp, Lewis and Clark keep the men boiling seawater for salt.
They keep the men hunting, making clothes.

[Lewis]
Tuesday March 18th 1806
Drewyer was taken last night with a violent pain in his side. Capt Clark blead him. several of the men are complaining of being unwell. it is truely unfortunate that they should be sick at the moment of our departure... Comowooll and two Cathlahmahs visited us today;

Lewis and Clark look for what the men can do to occupy themselves through the long winter.

You watch Lewis sit with his journals, his black letters, his white words.
His writing gets him through.

Lewis and Clark leave notes as evidence of their arrival at the mouth of the Columbia. Maybe a ship will take news back to their President, the one with the *petite chienne* and the magpie singing in his office.

Maybe Lewis and Clark have been forgotten. Maybe the President does not think of them. Maybe he looks at them without seeing.

we suffered them to remain all night. this morning we gave Delashelwilt a certificate of his good deportment &c. And also a list of our names... with pre-amble... "The object of this list is, that through the medium of some civilized person who may see the same, it may be made known to the informed world, that the party consisting of the persons whose names are here-unto annexed, and who were sent out by the government of the U'States in May 1804. to explore the interior of the con-tinent of North America did penetrate the same by way of the Missouri and Columbia Rivers, to the discharge of the latter into the Pacific Ocean, where they arrived on the 14th of November 1805, and from there they departed on the day of March 1806 on their return to the United States..."

The explorers prepare to leave the Killamucks, Clatsops, Chinooks, Cathlahmahs, Wackiacums.
Lewis makes notes on their dress, their hair and skin, their habits.

Rain and wind delay the explorers.
Willard and Bratten are still sick.

Finally, one afternoon, you leave Fort Clatsop. You see Lewis looking forward on the river. You do not look back.

Seaman barks into the wind.

At one point, there is an Indian canoe on shore. Lewis takes it without asking. Is this Lewis who steals again?

[Clark]
Sunday 23rd March 1806
This morning proved so raney and uncertain that we were undetermined for some time whether we had best set out & risque the [tide] which appeared to be riseing or not. Jo Colter returned having killed an Elk... the rain seased and it became fair about Meridian, at which time we loaded our canoes & at 1 P.M. left Fort Clatsop on our homeward bound journey. at this place we had wintered and remained from the 7th of Decr 1805 to this day and have lived as well as we had any right to expect, and we can say that we were never one day without 3 meals of some kind a day either pore Elk meat or roots, notwithstanding the repeated fall of rain which has fallen almost constantly since... Nov last...

The civilized acts like a savage?
Then can the savage act like a *civilized*.

As you ascend the Columbia River, the Wah-clel-lars throw stones at the men trying to pull the canoes up a steep bluff.

Later they decoy Seaman, leading him with pieces of meat. He follows until they have a rope around him.

Captain Lewis is in a rage over his dog, Seaman.
Lewis sends his men to retrieve him.

[Lewis]
Friday April 11th 1806
...Three of this same tribe of villains the Wah-clel-lars, stole my dog this evening, and took him towards their village; I was shortly afterwards informed of this transaction by an indian who spoke the Clatsop language... and sent three men in pursuit of the theives with orders if they made the least resistence or difficulty in surrendering the dog to fire on them; they overtook these fellows or reather came within sight of them at the distance of about 2 miles; the indians discovering the party in pursuit left the dog and fled...

The men chop up canoes for firewood when they have to portage.

The hills are steep. A pack horse carrying ammunition falls from the top into the creek, but is not hurt. It is the ghost horses helping him land.

The Indians still come to Lewis and Clark to be treated for their diseases.

There is a woman with a large boil on her back. Lewis lances and drains it.

While at dinner, an Indian throws a poor half starved puppy at Lewis, who throws it back, hitting him in the chest and face. Lewis grabs his tomahawk and says he will kill the Indian if he does it again. The puppy lays dazed on the floor.

A Shoshoni guide with Neeshneparkeeook, or Cut Nose, tells Lewis and Clark that snow is on the Rocky Mountains until the next full moon, or even the first of June.
You know the disappointment of the explorers. You also want to eat the buffalo of the plains.

Do they think a river flows one way, then the other? Don't they know there has to be mountains between them to drive the water in the other direction? To drive the course of the river into the sea to keep the sea from coming into the river with its salt? Both the river and the land have to push it back.

You think there must be salt water down river from the Missouri. Why else

[Clark]
Wednesday May 7th 1806
...The Indians inform us that the snow is yet so deep on the mountains that we shall not be able to pass them untill after the next full moon or about the first of June. others set the time at a more distant period... this was unwelcom inteligence to men confined to... horsebeef and roots, and who are anxious to return to the fat plains of the Missouri, and thence to our native homes...

would it flow past the Mandan village the way it does?
You wonder about the shape of the land.

Toussaint looks at the Chopunnish deer heads which they use to decoy deer when they cannot follow them through the woods on horses.

Seaman catches a small deer close to camp.

[Lewis]
Thursday 8th of May 1806
...The Snake Indian was much displeased that he was not furnished with as much Deer as he could eate. he refused to speake to the wife of Shabono, through whome we could understand the nativs. we did not indulge him and in the after part of the day he came too and spoke very well...

[Clark]
Wednesday May 14th 1806
we have found our stonehorses [stallions] so troublesome that we indeavoured to exchange them with the Chopunnish for mears or gel[d]ings but they will not excha[n]ge altho' we offer 2 for one, we came to a resolution to castrate them and began the operation this evening one of the Indians present offered his services on this occasion. he cut them without tying the string of the stone as is usual, and assures us that they will do much better in that way...

[Lewis]
Saturday May 17th 1806
It rained the greater part of the last night and this morning until 8 OCk the water passed through [the] flimzy covering and wet our bed most perfectly in sho[r]t we lay in the water all the latter part of the night... I opened it [the chronometer] and founded [it] nearly filled with water which I carefully drained out exposed it to the air and wiped the works as well as I could with dry feathers after which I touched them with a little bears oil. several parts of the iron and steel works were rusted a little which I wiped with all the care in my power. I set her to going and from her apparent motion hope she has sustained no material injury... I am pleased at finding the river rise so rapidly, it no doubt is attributeable to the me[l]ting snows of the mountains; that icy barier which seperates me from my friends and Country, from all which makes life esteemable— patience, patience...

[Clark]
Sunday 18th May 1806
...The Squar wife of Shabono busied her self gathering the roots of the fenel called by the Snake Indians Year-pah for the purpose of drying to eate on the Rocky mountains.

A line of people still stand outside Lewis's tent.

They have come to see these traveling medicine men.

They should not bother them with their complaints.

[Lewis]
Monday May 19th 1806
...at 11 A.M. Thompson returned from the village accompanyed by a train of invalids consisting of 4 men 8 women and a child. The men had soar eyes and the women in addition had soar eyes had a variety of other complaints principally rheumatic; a weakness and pain in the loins is a common complaint with their women... eyewater was administered to all; to two of the women cathartics were given, to a third who appeared much dejected and who from their account of her disease we supposed to be histerical, we gave 30 drops of Laudanum...

Frazier, J. Fields, and Wiser have pains in their heads. Howard and York have pains in their stomach. Others are not well. They should busy themselves and not be sick.

Lewis treats a chief who cannot walk. He is not in pain, and there is no cause for his sickness. Lewis gives him cream of tartar and sulphur, a few drops of Laudanum and a little portable soup, and tells him to take a cold bath.

Jean Baptiste cries at anything. He is irritable. He cries to cry. None of the men can make him laugh.

Now he feels warm.

Jean Baptiste is sick. His jaw and neck are swollen. You rock him. He has fever. You try to cool him.

[Lewis]
Thursday May 22nd 1806
...Charbono's Child is very ill this evening; he is cuting teeth, and for several days past has a violent lax, which having suddonly stoped he was attacked with a high fever and his neck and throat are much swollen this evening. we gave him a doze of creem of tartar and flour of sulpher and applyed a poltice of boiled onions to his neck as warm as he could bear it...

You take John Baptiste to Lewis.

[Clark]
Thursday 22nd May 1806
...Shabonos son a small child is dangerously ill. his jaw and throat is much swelled. we apply a poltice of onions, after giveing him some creem of tartar &c. This day proved to be fine and fair which afforded us an oppertunety of drying our baggage which had got a little wet.

You pray to your mother and father in the next world. You tell them to keep Jean Baptiste in this world.

You hold him to yourself.
You are afraid the ghost horses will take him.

You feel your stone heart.
It is a white lump in your chest.
You feel it beat.

[Lewis]
Saturday May 24th 1806
The child was very wrestless last night; it's jaw and the back of it's neck are much more swollen than they were yesterday tho' his fever has abated considerably. We gave it a doze of creem of tartar and applyed a fresh poltice of onions...

You think of Otter Woman. There are thoughts that travel over the distance. You tell her Jean Baptiste is sick. You ask her help.

[Lewis]
Sunday May 25th 1806
...the Child is more unwell than yesterday. We gave it a doze of creem of tartar which did not operate, we therefore gave it a clyster in the evening...

You tell Jean Baptiste stories of Beaverhead.
You tell him of the long journey he still has to make.

His lips chatter like the birds.

You plead with Lewis and Clark.
You plead with the Maker.

You ask the Maker for a dream so you will know what will
happen, but no dream comes.

What would you do with Jean Baptiste?

Toussaint cries and is inconsolable.

Does Jean Baptiste see the animal spirits?
Does he see the buffalo with stars on his hind legs?
The elk with a moon on his back?
The bear who has a snow storm in its mouth?
The badger with a lightning bolt tail?
The porcupine carrying a cloud?

Are his spirit animals smaller than he is?

Because there is no dream,
you think Jean Baptiste
will heal.

> [Lewis]
> Tuesday May 27th 1806
> ...Charbono's son is much better
> today, tho' the swelling on the
> side of his neck I believe will ter-
> minate in an ugly imposthume a
> little below the ear.

He cries when he tries to suck.
You squeeze your milk into his mouth.
He cries when he swallows.
He chokes and you pat him on the back.
Then you try again.

You rock him and sing him a song to live.

When he does, you thank
the Maker.

[Lewis]
Wednesday May 28th 1806
...The child is also better, he is
free of fever, the imposthume is
not so large but seems to be
advancing to maturity...

[Clark]
Thursday 29th of May 1806
No movement of the party to
day worthy of notice... Bratten
is recovering his strength very
fast. the Child, and the Indian
Cheaf are also on the recovery.
The Chief has much more use
of his hands and arms... Since
my arrival here I have killed
several birds of the Corvus
genus of a kind found only in
the rocky mountains...

The men collect goat hair to stuff the saddles of their
horses so they won't ache
as much from riding.

[Lewis]
Friday May 30th 1806
...all our invalids are on the
recovery. we gave the sick Chief
a severe Swet to day, shortly
after which he could move one
of his legs and thy's and work
his toes... The reptiles which I
have which I have observed in
this quarter are rattle snake of
the species discribed on the
Missouri, they are abundant...

Lewis makes the likeness
of a bird with his words.
You are called Bird Woman.
Does he write you on his
page?

Why does he draw the
bird?
Not for power. Not to
honor.
But to copy its likeness?
To separate its parts?

[Lewis]
Friday June 6th 1806
...we met with a beautiful little
bird in this neighbourhood about
the size and somewhat the shape
of the large sparrow. it is rather
longer in proportion to it's bulk
than the sparrow. it measures 7
inches from the extremity of the
beek to that of the tail, the latter
occupying 2 1/2 inches. the beak
is reather more than half an inch
in length, and is formed much
like the virginia nitingale; it is
thick and large for a bird of its
size; wide at the base, both chaps
convex, and pointed, the uper
exceeds the under chap a little is
somewhat curved and of a brown
colour; the lower chap of a
greenish yellow... the eye full
raether large and of a black
colour both puple and iris. the
plumage is remarkably delicate;
that of the neck and head is of a
fine orrange yellow and red, the
latter predominates on the top of
the head and arround the base of
the beak from whence it graduly
deminishes & towards the lower
part of the neck, the orrange yellow prevails most; the red has the
appearance of being laid over a
ground of yellow. the breast,
the sides, rump and some of the
long feathers which lie between
the legs and extend underneath

the tail are of a fine orrange yellow. the tail, back and wings are
black, e[x]cept a small strip of
yellow on the outer part of the
middle joint of the wing, 1/4 of
an inch wide and an inch in
length. the tail is composed of
twelve feathers of which those in
the center are reather shortest,
and the plumage of all the feathers of the tail is longest on that
side of the quill next the center of
the tail... [&c. &c. &c........]

[Clark]
Sunday June 8th 1806
...The Sick Chief is much
mended, he can bear his weight
on his legs and recovers strength.
the Child has nearly recovered.

Jean Baptiste smiles again for the men.

You want to poke in the redroot, chockcherry, alder, shoe-
mate, sevenbark, purple haw, service berry, honeysuckle,
wild rose, gooseberry,
fir, pine, dwarf pine, larch,
&c.
You make *lists* of them in your thoughts.
You poke behind the stars, the sky.

[Lewis]
Thursday June 12th 1806
All our hunters except Gibson returned about noon; none of them had killed any thing except Shields who brought with him two deer... Musquetors... very troublesome... The Cutnose informed us... two young Chiefs would overtake us with a view to accompany us to the Falls of the Missouri... our camp is agreeably situated in a point of timbered land... the quawmash [camas] is now in blume at a Short distance it resembles a lake of fine clear water...

[Lewis]
Friday June 13th 1806
...about noon seven of our hunters returned with 8 deer; they had wounded several others and a bear but did not get them. in the evening Labuish and Cruzatte returned and reported that the buzzards had eaten up a deer which they had killed butchered and hung up this morning. The Indian who visited us yesterday exchanged his horse for one of ours which had not perfectly recovered from the operation of castration and received a small ax and a knife to boot...

Lewis and Clark have difficulty in finding their way. The snow nearly covers your legs. You can hardly walk. Your feet and hands are numb. The men build a scaffolding to store their baggage, and make a *retrograde* march to the camp they left. Even Seaman broods.

> [Lewis]
> Monday June 16th 1806
> ...Hungry creek is but small at this place... runs a perfect torrent; the water is perfectly transparent and as cold as ice. The pitch pine, white pine some larch and firs consti[tu]te timber... and the white cedar not further than the branch of hungry creek on which we dined.

You are able to travel again. You camp with some Indians.

You see Indians wearing clam shells tied with rawhide thongs around their necks for snow goggles.

You hold Jean Baptiste to watch the fire the Indians set in the trees.

> [Lewis]
> Wednesday June 25th 1806
> last evening the indians entertained us with seting the fir trees on fire. they have a great number of dry lims near their bodies which when set on fire creates a suddon and immense blaze from bottom to top of those tall trees...

Jean Baptiste is still not himself and tires easily.

The fire is a ceremony for the explorers' journey. Fire scares the ghost horses. Fire is a passage for weather-in-which-to-journey.

You cross the Bitterroots with the men. Clark says, with *cold and hunger he will not forget.*

You hear the quiet roar of the mountains.
Seaman, the dog, killed an elk, yet the smaller beaver bit
him. You have made the journey, but it is the ghost horses
that will still bite you.

You camp at the hot
springs with the explorers.
The Indians have stopped
the stream with rocks to
make a pool.

It is a place where the sun
loses some of its leaves.
It is a place where friction
rubs blisters.

A place-where-the-sun
folds-into-the-earth.

You sit in the pool when
the men have run to the
cold creek.

[Lewis]
Sunday July 29th 1806
...we passed our encampment of
the (13th) September at 10 ms...
we found after we halted that one
of our pack-horses with his load
and one of my riding horses were
left behind. We dispatched J.
Fields and Colter in surch of the
lost horses... These warm springs
... on the N. Side and near the
bank of travellers rest creek...
issue from the bottoms and
through the interstices of...
rock... the prinsipal spring is
about the temperature of the
warmest baths used at the hot
springs in Virginia... I remained
in 19 minutes, it was with difficulty I could remain thus long and it
caused a profuse sweat two other
springs... were much warmer,
their heat being so great as to
make the hand of a person smart
extreemly when immerced...
both the men and indians amused
themselves with the use of a bath
this evening. I observed that the
indians after remaining in the hot
bath as long as they could bear it
ran and plunged themselves into
the creek the water of which is
now as cold as ice can make it;

after remaining here a few minutes they returned again to the warm bath, repeating this transision several times but always ending in the warm bath... I killed a small black pheasant... saw some young pheasants which were about the size of Chickens of 3 days old...

[Lewis]
Tuesday July 1st 1806
...from this place I determined to go with a small party by the most direct rout to the falls of the Missouri, there to leave Thompson McNeal and goodrich to prepare carriages and geer for the purpose of transporting the canoes and baggage over the portage, and myself and six volunteers to ascend Maria's river with a view to explore the country and ascertain whether any branch of that river lies as far north as Latd 50. and again return and join the party who are to descend the Missouri, at the entrance of Maria's river. I now called for volunteers to accompnay me on this rout, many turned out, from whom I scelected Drewyer the two Feildes, Werner, Frazier and Sergt Gass [accompany me] the other prt of the men are to proceed with Capt Clark to the head of Jefferson's river where we despoited sundry articles and left

The hunters return with two deer.
Shields continues to repair guns.
The Indian guides, in preparing to leave, give Lewis a name, *Yo-me-kol-lo-lick, the white bearskin folded.*
Lewis gives them medals.

Goodrich and McNeal have the pox which they contracted last winter from the Chinook women. When they reach the falls, Lewis tells them they can rest and treat themselves with *murcury.*

our canoes. from hence Sergt Ordway with a party of 9 men are to decend the river with the canoes; Capt C. with the remaining including Charbono and York will proceed to the Yellowstone river at it's nearest approach to the three forks of the missouri, here he will build a canoe and decend the Yellowstone river with Charbono the indian woman, his servant York and five others to the missouri where should he arrive first he will wait my arrival. Sergt Pryor with two other men are to proceed with the horses by land to the Mandan and thence to the British posts on the Assinniboin with a letter to Mr. Heney [Haney]...

This day the explorers split into four groups to go their different ways. Lewis will shortcut overland to the Great Falls. Clark will go to the Yellowstone and the others &c.

It will be a month before you are together again.

Seaman paces one way, then another. He is confused as you leave. The men have split before into bands, but maybe he has forgotten. Maybe it is Jean Baptiste he doesn't want to leave.

[Clark]
Tuesday July 3rd 1806
We colected our horses and after brackfast I took My leave of Capt. Lewis and the indians and at 8 A M Set out with Men interpreter Shabono & his wife & child... for the Crow Inds and the latter for the Shoshoni... I observed 2 Species of Clover... after letting our horses graze a Sufficient length of time to fill themselves, and taking dinner of venison we again resumed our journey...

He will be all right, you tell Seaman.

Clark takes a twelve-man detachment: Pryor, Scannon, Bratton, Hall, Windsor, Shields, Gibson, Labiche, York, Toussaint, Jean Baptiste, and Sacajawea (you).

[Lewis]
[Sacajawea was not with Lewis when he made the following note]
July 5th 1806
...[in mapping their route] East 3 M. to the entrance of a large creek 20 yds wide Called Seaman's Creek...

The night is cold. You cannot sleep. Jean Baptiste stays in his sack where it is warm. But he is not quiet.

He turns and kicks all night.
He is like laying beside a pulsing star.
He is like sleeping with a sack full of stars.

You pass overland on horse-

[Clark]
Sunday 6th July 1806
...in every direction around which I could see high points of Mountains covered with snow... The Squar pointed to the gap through which she said we must pass... she said we would pass the river before we reached the gap...

back. You see Clark looking at the mountains. You see the pass you used to cross with the Shoshoni. You point it out to Clark. He listens to what you say. He leads the men toward the pass, a journey of several days.

A tail of rain comes down from the sky.

You gather quawmash and give it to Clark.

You think the jaw and neck of Jean Baptiste are still tender.

At Beaverhead, the men find their cache, with canoes and the supply of tobacco the men are crazy for, still intact.
You remember the cache in the Mandan lodges. You remember the squash rings and dried ears of corn. You feel your ache.

You will travel by horse until Clark can find timber to make canoes.

The mosquitoes are an evil spirit. They sweep across you with their sleeve.

> [Clark]
> Wednesday 9th July 1806
> ...The Squar brought me a plant the root of which the nativs eat...

> [Clark]
> Sunday 13th July 1806
> ...The indian woman who has been of great service to me as pilot through this country recommends a gap in the mountain more south which I shall cross...

The horses feet are sore from the stones and gravel. You help the men make moccasins from green skins.

Clark finds that some of his horses are gone. No one sees them, but the Indians are here.
Those Crows, those horse-takers.

You see the grasshoppers have eaten all the prairie grass. You see where buffalo cross the river.

You find the old Indian forts.
You explain them to Clark when he asks.
You remember hiding in the fort with your mother, but you do not tell him you remember your mother panting. You remember the sweat of her body. Her fear. You were small and you sat by her feet. You did not make a noise.

[Clark]
Thursday 17th July 1806
...I saw in one of those small bottoms which I passed this evening an Indian fort which appears to have been built last summer. this fort was built of logs and bark. the logs was put up very closely (ends supporting each other)... and closely chinked... the Squar informs me that when the war parties (of Minnit. Crows &c, who fight Shoshonees) find themselves pursued they make those forts to defend themselves in from the purusers whose superior numbers might otherwise over power them and cut them off without receiveing much injurey on horsback &c.

Toussaint's horse steps into a burrow and trips, throwing Toussaint over his head. You see Clark writing in his journal. You don't want him to write about Toussaint's fall. Another man, Gibson, falls while getting on his horse and a snag pierces his thigh. Clark dresses the wound. You know the man hurts. The next day when Gibson can no longer ride his horse, Sergt Pryor waits with him until he can ride again.

[Clark]
Friday 18th July 1806
...as we were about Setting out this morning two Buffalow Bulls came near our Camp. Several of the men shot at one of them. their being near the river plunged in and Swam across to the opposit Side and there died. Shabono was thrown from his horse to day in pursute of a Buffaloe... he is... brused on his hip sholder & face...

You see an Indian watching from the high lands. You point him out to Toussaint. That evening you see the smoke from their fires.
Clark sees it too.

One night, the wolves come into camp and eat the dried meat from a scaffolding. You think of Seaman. He would not have let the wolves come.

Clark wants the horses to be given to the Mandan.

You watch the men making canoes. You are nearing the Rockejhone [Yellowstone]. Clark will give the horses to the Indians. Shields and Labeech kill three buffalo. You save as much meat as the canoes can carry.

Now the men make the oars and poles.

You get into the dug-out canoes which are two cottonwood trees lashed together.

Now you are on the Yellowstone River. You passed here as a girl.

There are sandstone bluffs on the north side of the river. On the south, a single pillar stands by itself.

The pillar is a stone heart standing across the river from the cliffs on the north side of the Yellowstone. The pillar is a mountain-lion's heart. Clark tells you the river cut the pillar away from the cliffs, but you know the pillar was thrown by the spirits.

Clark names the rock *Pompey's Pillar.*

It is called the *Place-Where-the-Mountain-Lion-Dwells* by the Crow.

[Clark]
Friday 25th July 1806
...I proceeded on after the (rain) lay a little and at 4 P M arrived at a remarkable rock situated in an extensive bottom on the Stard Side of the river & 250 paces from it. this rock I ascended and from it's top had a most extensive view in every direction. This rock which I shall call Pompy's Tower is 200 feet high and 400 paces in secumpherance... The Indians have made 2 piles of stone on top of this Tower. The nativs had ingraved on the face of this rock the figures of animals &c. near which I marked my name and the day of the month and year... emense herd of Buffalow about our [camp]... the bulls keep such a grunting nois which is [a]very loud disagreeable sound that we are compelled to scear them away before we can sleep...

Clark writes his name on the rock.
You climb to the rock with Jean Baptiste and show him where Clark writes his name.
Jean Baptiste could write if he would go to school, Clark tells you.

Will Jean Baptiste be cut away from his people too? Jean Baptiste is as much of them as he is of you. Who are his people? He is Shoshoni and French. He lives-among-others-not-of-his-kind. He has become all of them.

You hear the birds, the water. Jean Baptiste picks up cottonwood fuzz, puts it under his nose.

You don't want that pillar named after Jean Baptiste. You want him to be with others of his kind. But you see Jean Baptiste is divided from the others. French Canadian, Shoshoni. He is Clark's *god son*, Clark says. You see in him three paths have come together. He is part of the men he travels with. It is their voices he hears. It is them who make his path.

Maybe that's why Jean Baptiste had a hard time being born. He carried so many with him.

He likes his cottonwood fuzz, like the soft fur close to an animal's breast.

At night, the buffalo snort. Jean Baptiste makes snoring noises like the buffalo. The men laugh. The buffalo keep snorting. Jean Baptiste keeps snorting. You think also Jean Baptiste remembers Seaman. The men shoot their guns to chase the buffalo away.

You sing a song for the three other detachments as they move toward the Yellowstone and Missouri rivers.

You remember Jean Baptiste at Pompey's Pillar. You think he will leave his people too. Look how Clark talks to him. *My boy, Pomp*, he calls him.
You think Jean Baptiste's clan father is William Clark.
You look at Toussaint to see if he is angry, but he does not know what you are thinking.

Clark names the next river Baptiste Creek.

Jean Baptiste is restless. He must sit in the boat. You give him a stick and he rows.
He walks back to you. He stands with other men who talk to him as they row until he gets in their way.
Toussaint yells at him to sit. He yells at you to hold him.
You want Jean Baptiste to be like Clark. You want him to have patience. Fortitude. Resolve.

If you had buffalo bones he could play with them.

In the evening, you give him chewed meat.

Toussaint will tie him to his seat—
But if the dug-out overturns, he will be held under—
Dug-outs tied together will not overturn—
But if they do—
Make him a float from an elk's stomach. Make him a float from buffalo lungs
or the heart skin of a buffalo.

The men say they will save him.

In the evening, you pass a bend in the Yellowstone. The bluffs follow. Sometimes they look like Indian villages. You think the ancestors line up to watch you pass. As soon as you turn the bend, they go back to the other world.

The river is bumpy as the moon.

At night, you see the shadows of its villages.
The buttes and valleys on the moon.

You sing a song of the day's occurrences. Just as Clark writes. Singing is another way of writing. You want Jean Baptiste to know this way of speaking.
A song: a fine day &c.

Now you hear the high whine of mosquitoes. The buzz of the flies. You hear the insect voices. You hear the song of the fish. The sound of the land.

But now the mosquitoes attack. The men try to cover themselves with their blankets, but they are worn and full of holes.

[Clark]
Wednesday 4th August 1806
Musquetors excessively troublesom so much so that the men complained that they could not work at their Skins for those troublesom insects. and I find it entirely impossible to hunt in the bottoms... our best retreat from those insects is on the Sand bars in the river... The child of Shabono has been so much bitten by the Musquetors that his face is much puffed up & Swelled...

You try to beat them off Jean Baptiste. They must have bitten him while you slept. His face swells. His face does not look like him.

On the river, Jean Baptiste rocks against you as you row. There is a small buffalo hide from Lewis's failed boat that he sleeps on. You sing him a song. You shade him from the sun when he sleeps. You fan the mosquitoes away. He cries when his cottonwood fuzz blows away.

You pick up more the next stop.

You see him already trying to be like them. What will he do when they row on? Does he know it is coming? Does he think it will always be this way?

You feel something in your throat. It is the stone heart you swallow. You have been with them for two winters and two summers. Do you think this will go on? Don't you know you will be left?

The last time you passed along this way, you and Otter Woman had been taken from the Shoshoni and were traveling northeast with the Hidasta. You were afraid and she would comfort you.

Maybe another man has taken her. Maybe she waits. Maybe she is dead.

You pass:
Bighorn River.
Tongue River.
Powder River.
O'Fallon Creek.

You hear the Indian voices as a flock of birds from the old world.
You hear the new world in Jean Baptiste.

His world is still in the distance with the hills.

In a dream a man on a horse rides up, says something, rides off again. But you don't know what he said. You knew when you slept, but now you are awake and you can't remember. Maybe it will come.

You row with the current. The dugouts move swiftly downsteam.

The men hunt black tailed deer and grouse.

You are afraid of what is ahead.

If you had to say what the man said, you would say the animals will be gone. Even the trees. But you cannot believe that's what he said.

Now the four parties of explorers come together again.

Samah! Jean Baptiste says. Lewis's dog sits by Lewis in the boat.

You see Lewis has been shot. Cruzatte mistook his buckskin for a deer and shot him through the hip. He will be all right, he tells Clark. Just give him time to recover.

[Clark]
Thursday 12th August 1806
...at Meridian Capt Lewis hove in Sight with the party which went by way of the Missouri as well as that which accompanied him from Travelers rest... I was alarmed on the landing of the Canoes to be informed that Capt Lewis was shot by accident. I found him lying in the Perogue, he informed me that his wound was slight and would be well in 20 or 30 days...

You pull back from Lewis.
You see a ghost horse standing by him.

Clark pets Seaman. Lewis tells him how Seaman cried with mosquito bites.
Even the horses stood in the smoke of the fires.

Lewis, who had hoped Maria's River would connect to the Saskatchewan, was disappointed it did not.

That night you see the moon. When it is full, it is a white mound lodge.

You hear the men talk. Lewis tells Clark they killed two Indians. Blackfeet. Lewis says the explorers rode in flight two days without stopping. You listen, but you do not say anything.

You come to the Mandan village.

You see the earth lodges, hairy with grasses growing upon them in the summer. You see the buffalo-hump village, the many-prairie-dog village, the beaver-mound-village. You think of names for the village. If you were one of the explorers-who-name, you could call it Jean-Baptiste's-village. You could call it Jean-Baptiste-and-Toussaint-Charbonneau's village. You could call it Toussaint-Charbonneau-his-wives-and-children's village.

The Indians stand on the bank to meet you.
Otter Woman is among them.

You see corn from the green-corn harvest drying on the scaffolding between lodges built close together.
In one month, Otter Woman and you will harvest the ripe corn with them.

All the voices in the village speak as one with the wind and the birds.
You want Jean Baptiste to hear.
You see a black and a white butterfly.
Grasses flattened where animals had slept in the night.

You hear the owl.
The prairie hen with a sharp click for a cry.

You hear the ceremonial song to catch fish in the willow
fish traps.

You see the buffalo berry bush you will pick.
Jean Baptiste will help.

In the winter, Otter Woman and you will bead, weave
baskets, and make pottery from river clay.
You will tell her of the journey you made with the
explorers.
There is much that separates you. You will cross the
journey back to her.
You will tell her of the Shoshoni village.

In spring, when there are leaves of the wild gooseberry
bushes (which are the first to bloom), Otter Woman and
you will plant corn with a buffalo-shoulder-bone-hoe.
You will sit on the platform to hiss away the birds.
You will make a scarecrow from cast-off skin of an old
robe.
You will sing to the spirit of the corn.

Otter Woman and you will make a round bull boat with
the green hide of a buffalo.

[Clark]
Thursday August 15th 1806
Mandan Vilg.
after assembling the Chiefs and
Smokeing one pipe, I informed
them that I still Spoke the
Same words which we had
Spoken to them when we first
arived in their Country in the
fall of 1804. we then envited
them to visit their great father
the president of the U. States
and to hear his own Councils
and receive his Gifts from his
own hands us also See the pop-
ulation of a government which
can be at their pleasure protect
and Secure you from all your
enemies, and chastize all those
who will shut their years to his
Councils...

There is an Indian who opens his heart, the son of a chief.
He says he sees the heart of Lewis and Clark.
Are they born with a higher spirit? Do they learn it?
Does the Maker speak to them? Does he make them see?

You see the Maker speaks differently to Lewis than Clark.
You see more than you know.

Lewis and Clark say they want peace among the Indians.

But there will be no peace with the Indians. Raiding and warfare are a ritual.

Without war, what would they do for chiefs?

Without war, how would honor be achieved?

The Indian see these explorers are different from fur traders who sell everything they have.

What is it Lewis and Clark have?

A heart skin?

A sacredness of behavior?

What is their word for it?

Do they have it because it gets them where they want to go? Or is it for its own sake?

These men-who-know-the-way-where-they-have-not-been.

They have a source for what they are.

You want it.

[Clark]

Saturday 17th August 1806

a cool morning gave some powder & Ball to Big White Chief Settled with Touisant Charbono for his services as an enterpreter the price of a horse and Lodge purchased of him for public Service in all amounting to 500$ 33 1/3 cents... we also took leave of T. Chabono, his Snake Indian wife and their child [son] who had accompanied us on our rout to the pacific ocean... T. Charbono wished much to accompany us in the said Capacity if we could have provailed [upon] the Menetarre Chiefs to dec[e]nd the river with us to the U. States, but as none of those Chiefs of whose language he was Conversent would accompany us, his services were no longer of use to the U. States and he was therefore discharged and paid up. we offered to convey him down to the Illinois if he chose to go, he declined proceeding on at present, observing that he had no acquaintance or prospects of makeing a liveing below, and must continue to live in the way that he had done. I offered to take his little son a butifull promising child who is 19 months old to which they both himself & his wife wer willing provided the child had

You want it for Jean Baptiste.

been weened. they observed that in one year the boy would be sufficiently old to leave his mother & he would then take him to me if I would be so friendly as to raise the child for him in such a manner as I thought proper, to which I agreed &c...

Colter, one of the explorers, leaves the men. He wants to go upriver and trap.
He will not return to St. Louis.

At the Mandan village, Lewis and Clark leave guns, powder, balls, canon, for the Mandans to defend themselves against their enemies. They ask if the Mandan chief wants to accompany them to the seat of their government. The chief does not want to go because the Sioux would kill him as he returned up the Missouri River.

Toussaint wants to continue to translate, but it is Jessaume, his wife and two children, who go down river with Lewis and Clark. It is Jessaume now who speaks the language they need.

You have seen the-ones-who-come.

The ones whose-idea-of-journey-is-more-than-their-fear-of-it.

When Lewis and Clark leave, Seaman sits in the boat lapping the wind.

You turn away. You do not look back.

When they are gone, the day is an empty bull boat.

You make bone fishhooks. You pick chokecherries. You gather firewood. You make medicine bundles with sacred roots.

You see the Indians throw sticks into the river. They believe the sticks will return in the spring as buffalo.

Sometimes in the night you feel your fever. You feel the *Bad Medicine* the explorers bring.
Sometimes you hear the ghost horses.

Holy Maker.
Holy God.

Mon Dieu.
You remind Toussaint that William Clark saved his life the summer he was caught in the river and would have drowned.
You tell him Clark can help Jean Baptiste also.

When Jean Baptiste is six years old, Toussaint and you take him to St. Louis and leave him with William Clark. You hear that Lewis has died. You remember your dream of his ghost horse.

After you return from St. Louis, a girl is born. Toussaint and you name her Lizette.

You bead a doll for Lizette, but you hear the birds. You think of the bravery and endurance of Lewis and Clark.

You think of Jean Baptiste. You feel your longing for him.

The evenings grow darker.
The fever returns.

You dream of the white stone beaver heart.

You dream of the white stone beaver
without a tail,
with short dull teeth.

Now you dream again.
You see the stone beaver has long teeth.
You see it turn toward the river.
You see its tail.

hey hey hey
hey hey hey hey hi

[John C. Luttig, clerk at Fort Manuel, North Dakota]
this evening Dec 20, 1812, the wife of Charbonneau a Snake Squaw, died of a putrid fever. She was a good and best woman in the fort. Aged abt 25 years she left a fine infant Girl.

[Clark, when listing members
of the party]
1820
Se car ja we au Dead

It is possible Sacajawea died of
diphtheria.

It is possible Sacajawea died of
syphilis.

President Thomas Jefferson's instructions to Captain Meriwether Lewis

June 20, 1803
In all your intercourse with the natives, treat them in the most friendly and conciliatory manner which their own conduct will admit. Allay all jealousies as to the object of your journey. Satisfy them of its innocence. Make them acquainted with the position, extent, character, peaceable and commercial dispositions of the U.S., of our wish to be neighborly, friendly and useful to them, and of our dispositions to a commercial intercourse with them. Confer with them on the points most convenient as mutual emporiums, and articles of most desirable interchange for them and us. If a few of their influential chiefs within a practicable distance wish to visit us, arrange such a visit with them and furnish them with authority to call on our officers on their entering the U.S. to have them convey to this place at public expense. If any of them should wish to have some of their young people brought up with us, and taught such arts as may be useful to them, we will receive, instruct and take care of them. Such a mission whether of influential chiefs or young people would give some security to your own party. Carry with you some manner of the *kennepox*. Inform those of them with whom you may be of its efficacy as a preservative from the smallpox, and instruct and encourage them in the use of it. This may be especially done wherever you winter. As it is impossible for us to foresee in what manner you will be received by those people, whether with hospitality or hostility, so it is impossible to prescribe the exact degree of perseverance with which you are to pursue your journey. We value too

much the lives of citizens to offer them to probable destruction. Your numbers will be sufficient to secure you against the unauthorized opposition of individuals or of small parties, but if a superior force, authorized or not authorized by a nation, should be arrayed against your further passage, and inflexibly determined to arrest it, you must decline its further pursuit and return. In the loss of yourselves, we should lose also the information you will have acquired. By returning safely with that, you may enable us to renew the essay with better calculated means. To your own discretion, therefore, must be left the degree of danger you may risk and the point at which you should decline. Only saying we wish you to err on the side of your safety and bring back your party safe, even if it be with less information.

Afterword

[Clark]
September 25th
A fine morning we commenced wrighting &c.

In 2001 and 2002, on four different occasions, I drove by myself along different parts of the Lewis and Clark expedition, from the mouth of the Missouri River above St. Louis, Missouri, to the mouth of the Columbia River on the Pacific coast in Oregon. I also drove up Lemhi pass in the Idaho Bitterroot Mountains on a dirt road that climbed to 7,373 feet. I listened to the Lewis and Clark journals on tape as I drove and wrote Sacajawea's voice from the little they said about her, filling in the rest with research and imagination. Sometimes my experiences and the journals were eerily similar. When I got out of the car at Beaver's Head rock in Montana, I saw an immense bank of gray clouds in the distance. As I drove off, I listened to the storm Lewis and Clark encountered in the same place. I missed the rain only because I had a car in which to drive away.

No one agrees how to say or spell Sacajawea's name. It has been spelled Sacagawea and Sakakawea. In Hidasta, her name was Tsi-ki-ka-si-as or Bird Woman. In Shoshoni her name meant Boat Pusher. Lewis spelled her name Se car ja we au and Sah-Sah-gar-we-ah. Clark spelled her name Sah-kah-gar we a and Sahcahgagwea. But Lewis and Clark, phonetic spellers, could spell a word a dozen ways. Their language was fluid as the river. Their expedition took place before Noah Webster standardized the English language with his dictionary.

Sacajawea did not speak English, but the story had to be written in English. In the beginning of my research, along I-70 in Missouri and I-29 in Iowa, I saw the remains of the old two-lane highways I had once driven on my way to Columbia when I was in college, and later, when my parents lived in Northern Iowa. I had the thought that the old way was still there, though the road had changed. Maybe the spirit of the language could still be there also. Maybe as I traveled over the land, I could find Sacajawea's voice.

I washed some water over the edge of the manuscript, *baptizing* it in the Missouri River, July 10, 2001, at Wolf Point, Montana.

I wanted to write about Sacajawea without the myth of her leadership. The only time she led the men was on the return trip, and that was after the Corps of Discovery had broken into four different groups and she remembered a pass her tribe had taken through the mountains. William Clark took her advice and the small group crossed what is now Bozeman Pass. But myth kept returning. At Decision Point, near the Great Falls in Montana, as I stood beside the Missouri River, I found a white rock and imagined the dream Sacajawea's grandmother had at her birth. Maybe the lesson is that myth is a necessary part.

If there is something that could be called the creative consciousness of a continent, it is in the land, which is a containment of the voices that have crossed it. It is where I picked up Sacajawea's voice. In the end, the writing is as much of a journey as the written.

Bibliography

Ambrose, Stephen, *Undaunted Courage*, Simon & Schuster, New York, 1996

Bakeless, John, *Lewis and Clark, Partners in Discovery*, William Morrow Co., New York, 1947

Cutright, Paul Russell, *Lewis and Clark: Pioneering Naturalists*, University of Illinois Press, Urbana, Illinois, 1969

DeVoto, Bernard, *The Journals of Lewis and Clark*, Books on Tape, Inc. Newport Beach, CA, 1983

Burns, Ken, and Duncan, Dayton, *Lewis & Clark, the Journey of the Corps of Discovery*, Random House Aud iobooks, New York, 1998

Howard, Harold P., *Sacajawea*, University of Oklahoma Press, Norman Oklahoma, 1977

Karwoski, Gail Langer, *Seaman, the Dog Who Explored the West with Lewis & Clark*, Peachtree Press, Atlanta, Georgia, 1999

Ronda, James, *Lewis and Clark among the Indians*, University of Nebraska Press, Lincoln, Nebraska, 1984

——, *Voyages of Discovery, Essay on the Lewis and Clark Expedition*, Montana Historical Society Press, Helena, Montana, 1998

Rowland, Della, *The Story of Sacajawea, Guide to Lewis and Clark*, Bantam Doubleday Dell Books for Young Readers, New York, 1989

Thomas, George, *Lewis and Clark Trail, the Photo Journal*, Pictorial Histories Publishing Company, Missoula, Montana, 2000

Thwaites, Reuben Gold, LL.D. *Original Journals of the Lewis and Clark Expedition*, 10 volumes, Antiquarian Press Ltd. New York, 1959

Acknowledgments

Ron Laycock, Lewis & Clark Trail Heritage Foundation, for valuable information, and two articles, "Sacagawea and the Suffragettes," by Ronald Taber, and "The Sacajawea of Eva Emery Dye," by Ron Laycock, explaining the origin of the myth of Sacajawea as guide for the Lewis & Clark expedition (i.e. Eva Emery Dye and Grace Raymond Hebard in 1902, looking for heroines to advance their cause, chose Sacajawea to lift above what was historically accurate.)

Clem Guthro, Macalester College Library, for valuable assistance.

Dave Hall for the Photo Journal.

Mark Wiggs for his careful reading of the manuscript.

Jim Schaap for information on which forts to visit and the loan of the Ambrose book.

Chris Dantic at the Lewis & Clark Interpretive Center, Great Falls, Montana.

Also the Fort Mandan and Knife River Interpretive Centers in North Dakota, and Slant Village at Fort Lincoln near Bismarck.

Pompey's Tower Interpretive Center on the Yellowstone River in Montana, and Fort Clatsop near Astoria, Oregon.

River Oak Library, Chicago, Illinois, for a first reading of the manuscript, June 4, 2001.

Red Eye Theater, Minneapolis, Minnesota, for the Works-in-Progress Series, during which twenty minutes of the manuscript was performed, February 1-3, 2002.

Stone Heart was developed in part with support from the Playwright's Center, Many Voices Artist-in-Residence Program, Minneapolis, Minnesota.

And once again, acknowledgment to Macalester College for a Wallace Faculty Research Grant.